J I GRECO

GREED SLOTH ARROGANCE AND SHAME

WHOLESALE ATOMICS

ISBN (Paperback): 978-1-964666-09-9
ISBN (E-Book): 978-1-964666-19-8

Published by Wholesale Atomics.

Contents

One

MONDO HEETZE

THE FIRST THING MOST people do when they wake up in their new immortal bodies is go bungee-jumping.

Me, I took a nap. Then I rolled around on the floor for a bit–a nice cold linoleum hospital room floor, mind you. Then I tried to get someone to play fetch with me.

It was when I started drinking out of the toilette that I got around to wondering why I had been behaving so... unexpectedly.

Something was wrong. The toilette thing was the first clue. The extra arms were the second.

The room had a mirror, above the bureau. I hopped up on the bed to see.

I'd looked more human. Much more human. But not in a good way.

Four arms, short from shoulder to elbow but with forearms three times, proportionately, as long. Each arm was capped with a three-digit hand, each finger opposed to the other two in a sort of triangle arrangement. The fingers were thick, three-knuckled, and padded with rough callous-like skin. Sure, I had two legs, but they were physically much like my new arms, except more muscular. And I had a tail. A big, thick brute of a tail that just reached to the floor. The end of the tail was calloused, almost flat. I leaned back on it. It supported my weight quite comfortably, which was a good thing, since my new body wasn't exactly made for sitting in human chairs.

Okay, so the body was odd. But what really threw me was my neck and head. The neck was long, as long as the tail, and fairly flexible. I could turn my head to look behind me. Hell, I could look at my own ass—why I'd want to, couldn't tell you. My head was bulbous and alien: An oval on a stalk. Big black eyes, mouth behind and below the chin, teeth sharp, numerous, and small. Like a cat mated with a shark. No nose to speak of, though there were little slits running halfway down my neck, and I could breathe through them, and smell lunch being served two wings over.

To top everything off, I was covered with a mottled blue and yellow skin, textured like an elephant's. What hair I had was sparse, weak, and pale brown. It was thickest on my torso, which was stocky, with muscles moving under the skin in unfamiliar ways.

I recognized the type of creature my biodroid was modeled on, of course. You watch as much vid as I do, you're bound to see them, hanging at the heels—so to speak—of their enthak masters. Sometimes on leashes, most times not. They—or rather we, now—were considered quite intelligent and trainable pets. Not as trainable as humans, mind you, but in the eyes of the enthak at least, cuter.

They'd put me in the biodroid of a heetz. A damned pet.

Needless to say, I was incensed.

The attending technicians at the clinic were extremely apologetic. Seems the human-patterned biodroid body I had selected to spend at least the next thousand years in had been delivered from the factory in less than optimal condition. It had been missing a head, among other things. Naturally, they didn't notice until they'd already stripped my brain out of my original body.

They couldn't put me in the damaged biodroid, and they couldn't put me back in my own flesh. And since the nanochine fluid my brain was floating in would only keep my synapses alive for fourteen minutes, maximum, they didn't have much choice but to stick me in whatever was available.

The only empty biodroid at hand that a human's nervous system could handle integration with was a used heetz biodroid that had been on its way to becoming spare parts after its previous occupant traded up. Says something about the human nervous system, doesn't it, that hundreds of thousands of years of evolution had developed a system no more complex than an enthak pet.

They'd had empty enthak biodroids, but even if I could have afforded the upgrade, that would have been like putting a moped engine in a diesel train. Maybe it would power the whistle.

While the technicians were telling me this, I was sniffing their crotches.

They told me that kind of behavior would wear off. The neural net subsystems in the suit were overcompensating while my brain adjusted to its new digs, leaning on pre-programmed instincts. A normal effect of the transfer. Only problem was, the subsystems had been designed for a heetz, with a heetz's instincts.

I was going to tell them that I appreciated their concern, but that wasn't going to stop me from suing them, the clinic, the company that built the biodroid, the Consolidated Terran Overgovernment for allowing a company with such shoddy quality control to conduct business inside the solar system, and the enthak for introducing the biodroid technology in the first place.

Unfortunately, it came out as a short, friendly yip.

Then the moment was lost, and I went back to sniffing crotches.

The same afternoon as my release from the clinic, I had reported to the Personnel office of the Hershel-Sangrine Corporatti. If things had gone as planned I'd have been in a nice nearly-inde-structible human biodroid and immediately assigned a post on an asteroid-miner as a geologist/medic/general laborer. For thirty years. But that was nothing, considering that for that thirty years servitude my bills for the operation and the cost of the biodroid had been completely covered by Hershel-Sangrine, and after that I would have been free to live pretty much forever, doing what-ever I wanted. The key to all that was the human biodroid part. Something the Personal Director just couldn't grasp.

"You're contractually bound," he said from behind a bullet and laser proof transparent plastisteel shield that cut the room in half. I was on the side without air conditioning, but with loud piped-in elevator music.

"You can't be serious." My voice came out of a small, concealed speaker above my eyes–my biodroid mouth and tongue were good for growling and barking, not speaking Esperanto. "I'm not saying I'm not going to honor my obligations. Hell, no. Just delay the start. The clinic says they won't be able to put me in a new body–an actual human biodroid–for three months. My nervous system needs time to recover, build up some strength."

"I'm afraid we can't wait that long."

"I'm not exactly equipped–at the moment–to do the job."

"Hershel-Sangrine paid you a great deal of money."

"Yeah, but I paid for a human, not this damned thing." I raised my four arms in exasperation. "And I don't want to be stuck in it --"

"Not our problem. We made an investment, and the clinic tells me there's nothing "

"Of course they said that, they want me out of the way so I can't sue them."

"You can't sue them in any case." Expressionless, he touched a button on his desk to pop a holoflat up on the glass between us. I recognized the document in the flat–the thousand pages of microscopically small-printed contract with Hershel-Sangrine I'd signed and initialed in about a million places. "They are a wholly-owned subsidiary of Hershel-Sangrine, which you agreed to indemnify in all matters."

"Of course I did. Look–I can't even fit inside an EVA mining suit. Unless you've got one for heetz."

"I don't believe we do."

"That kind of makes my point, doesn't it? You've got to give me a few months."

"If you were still going to crew one of our belt ships, that might be the case. But mining isn't the only business Hershel-Sangrine is in. We also contract personnel out to other companies, and as luck would have it, a contract opportunity opened up just this morning."

"Is that so?" That's about when the sinking feeling I'd had the whole conversation became a full-fledge free-fall. "In this body?"

"You might say it's the perfect job for you."

My parents are in deep-freeze in a cryo-retirement home on Luna. It's a win-win kind'a thing, really. They're not really dead–just frozen in the last moment of life–so I never had to mourn them. And I don't have to visit them for the holidays. Win-win.

I bring this up not because it's a particularly unique thing, but because it vividly shows the effect of the enthak on humanity. The only hope my parents' generation had of achieving immortality was to submit to freezing, a questionable grab at the brass ring to be sure. But my generation, all we had to do was raise the cash for a biodroid and have our brain swapped in.

When the enthak made themselves known 17 years ago and revealed that they had been watching us, guiding our evolution, for nearly fifteen-hundred years, humanity was still fairly backwards technology wise. Couldn't even cure AIDS, we were in that sad a shape.

The enthak, on the other hand, there were about as advanced as they come. They'd been shepherding planets like earth for millennia to provide serfs for the various endeavors of their masters, the filanav–the race that created an empire by building massive interstellar tubeways for faster than light travel between their holdings. For the enthak, the technology of the biodroids was kindergarten stuff, and they gladly shared it with humanity. It was less a gift than a bribe, something to mollify the masses, a bit of misdirection while humanity was turned into a virtual slave-race.

But an immortal slave-race, for those who, like me, saw no real moral or ethical dilemma in taking the bribe. Life under the enthak wasn't much different from life before they came along, only the taxes were a little higher, and the news channels carried marginally more celebrity interviews and fewer political exposés. But we'd been heading that way on our own, anyway, so no loss there.

Anyway... if I were the sort of person who writes letters to dead people, I think my first letter home after getting to the enthak deep-space ship *Lkit* would have gone something like this:

"Dear Mom and Dad,

"Hope you haven't accidentally thawed since last we spoke.

"I'm doing well, except for the bit about being transplanted into a heetz. Bitch, that. Doesn't help I'm stuck in the damned thing for at least fifteen years. The boat I'm on won't be back in Earth's vicinity for that long, and I'm told not to count on the few ports of call we'll arrive at having facilities that can perform the operation, even if I had a human biodroid with me. The one I bought will be sitting in a warehouse in Houston collecting dust once the factory finishes it. Out of my reach. I'm gonna try not to think about it.

"You should see the ship your son has landed a job on. It's the largest thing I've ever seen. It isn't pretty, or in any way aesthetically pleasing, but at least it has raw size going for it.

"It doesn't look like a ship. It looks like someone took a palm tree, roots and all, and dipped it in tarnished bronze. It's seven miles long, and two miles wide at each end where the roots and branches spread themselves out. But inside, it's got everything you'd expect in a long-haul vessel. Labs, recreation facilities, its own marine detachment, and most importantly, actual artificial gravity.

"As for my job, it has nothing to do with geology. And I seriously doubt I'll have much opportunity to practice my medical skills–there is only one other human aboard, and she is in a biodroid. Human biodroid, of course. But you'll be pleased to hear I'm doing honest work.

"I catch rats.

"When I say rats, I mean alien rodents, not real rats. There're probably Terran rats somewhere aboard ship, but I haven't come across them yet. I've seen a couple dozen different species of alien rodent, from golf-ball sized Peg Betan tyrpes and eight-legged saracalobetes, to crocodile-like meffi and furry Lugren micrilatoes.

"I got the job because real heetz are natural-born rat catchers, or so they tell me. They get down and dirty. Like cats. But I can't allow myself to do that. Instead I've turned to the good old civilized standbys: Traps and poisons.

"I haven't rolled on the floor or taken a drink from a toilette since that first day in the clinic. I've sworn to myself that if the Fates have determined I am to spend my next few years in this body, I will at least deny them the pleasure of seeing me behave like an animal. I was a born a human–I am still a human, despite my body–and I refuse to give up my dignity, no matter how hard my new instincts tug at me.

"I think you can understand where I'm coming from. It's not really different in principle from that time the cable company raised the pay-per-view charge twice in the same month and Dad made us boycott TV for three days in protest. I only hope I can demonstrate that same strength of character.

"Anyway, time to go–my immediate supervisor, Nu Nu Ia, wants me to stop in to his office for a minute before my shift. I think he's going to give me a raise, or at least a certificate of commendation.

"Love, Jack.

"P.S. Did you get the electric blankets I sent for Kwanza?"

―――――――――――――

"You are not adequately performing your duties." That from Nu Nu Ia the second I entered his office.

I was flabbergasted. "What do you mean? I've bagged a ton."

He tentacles tapped his floating desk as his three giant oval eyes bore into me. "An average of two rodents a shift is hardly a ton, in any accepted measurement system. The other heetz averages ten."

"Yeah, well, he's a real heetz."

"Even the three-hundred year old robot averages four, and it is missing a wheel and it can only see green light."

"It's a trooper."

"Yes, it is. It actually hunts the rodents."

"I hunt the rodents," I protested.

"No, you set traps. And not particularly effective traps."

"I'm using the best traps on the ship. How can you say they aren't effective?"

"Would you like to see the surveillance recordings?"

"Recordings?"

"Observe." Nu Nu Ia slid to the left and pressed a power stud on the floor with a tentacle. One wall of the office revealed itself to be a giant holoflat. After a flicker of digital static an image of a trap I had set under a cluster of water and steam pipes resolved into focus. It was a traditional trap. A piece of processed cheese sat on the trigger, calling out to any passing rat-equivalent. In the upper right of the screen a time stamp rolled the hours away in fast forward.

The fast forward slowed to normal speed as a slight shadow fell over the trap. A second later a meffi crawled towards the trap. In its mouth it was carrying something furry. A dead tyrpe.

The meffi drew up to the trap, and with what I swear was deliberate calm, tossed the tyrpe on to the trap with a flick of its head.

The trap slammed down on the tyrpe.

After the trap settled down, the meffi crawled on top of it and started eating the cheese, and the parts of the tyrpe that weren't pinned under the bar.

Nu Nu Ia shut off the holoflat with the slap of a tentacle. "That is why we have heetz aboard. Because the rodents are too smart for traps."

"That meffi got lucky."

"No. Meffi are cunning. Most rodents are cunning. They must be hunted. Traps and tricks will not do."

"So you're saying you want me to hunt the rodents?"

"That is your job."

"You want me to crawl around on the floor, sniff for piss and shit trails, and then kill the things with my bare hands and teeth?"

"Yes."

"What do you think I am? Some kind of animal?"

"Of course."

I couldn't argue with that.

It took Nu Nu Ia two and a quarter hours to fully explain to me the heavy responsibilities of rat-catching and the importance of carrying my weight aboard ship. By the way he slid around and waved his tentacles at me accusingly he obviously took the whole thing seriously. Good for him. Annoying for me.

I spent the time squirming, nodding when I thought it appropriate by keying off his tone but pretty much ignoring the exact words Ia had to say. I took the opportunity to get lost in my own thoughts, and to have a solid wallow in self-pity, of course. A couple of times I even thought about telling Ia that a growing part of me did want to track and hunt rodents the old-fashioned animal way, but I wasn't about to give in to my new body's instincts that easily. Not for the enthak, not for the Hershel-Sangrine Corporatti, and certainly not for Nu Nu Ia. I had to maintain the human part of me as long as I could, and if that meant being thought of as a dead-weight employee, so be it.

After the lecture, I was in no mood to work so instead of going on shift I went to the mess hall for a sandwich and a few dozen beers. As luck would have it, Marilyn was there, getting drunk. Marilyn and I had bonded, at first because we were the only Terrans aboard, and then because it turned out we were both borderline alcoholics. For very different reasons–she enjoyed it (and her biodroid let her be really good at it), I needed it.

"I think she wants you," Marilyn said, pointing the bottom of a beer bottle over my shoulder.

I gagged on my pastrami and rye. "What?"

Across the mess hall a real heetz was sitting alone at a short table, sipping something from a bowl. It was a she, I knew that much. The skin on the top of her neck and back was thick with quills, indicating gender. She was a rat-catcher, too. The one with the exemplary performance record.

"See the way she's rolling on her heels?" Marilyn asked. "That's a classic heetz come-hither-I'm-horny gesture."

"I don't think so."

"'Tis true. Read it in a book. You're the one in the heetz body–haven't you done any research?"

"Why bother? The body's just a body. Inside I'm still human."

"Now that's not true, Jack. You're more than human. The neural networks interfacing your nervous system with the biodroid include programming to emulate the instincts of the model. That's hardwire, man."

"Hardwired, maybe. But suppressed. I'm valiantly ignoring them." Right. Despite the odd tingling in my inner thighs whenever I caught a glimpse of the way the female heetz swayed back and forth so enticingly. "Don't need 'em."

"Didn't say you need them. But you could use them." Marilyn smiled, sipped her beer. "Bet you can do a lot of fun shit in that body."

"Not interested." I forced myself to stop glancing over at the female heetz every other breath. Time to concentrate on finishing my sandwich and drinking my beer, not the biodroid-inspired illicit thoughts I couldn't stop my subconscious from entertaining, no matter how hard I tried.

"You're so pedestrian."

"And proud of it."

"Let me guess, you got your biodroid just to extend your life, right?"

"What other reason is there?"

"Life extension's the least of the benefits, Jack. We get to live forever, as long as we don't do something stupid like piloting a shuttle into a sun. Fine, great, but that's only the first step. We can live that eternity in a single body, one that duplicates exactly the body we were born with, but what does that get us? Nothing, except more of the same."

"Doesn't sound bad to me. Evolution designed a pretty good body when it did humans. I could do worse than spend eternity as a human. And once this tour is over, wild horses won't be able to stop me from getting in to the right biodroid."

"Yeah, but why not take advantage of it now—you're ahead of the game."

"What game?"

"The game only us eternals can play. The one where we spend a few decades as a human, then move on. Into a new body, a new species. Haven't you ever wondered what it would be like to run as a bull in Pamplona, or join a collective of Ierthian werewolves, or rut with a heetz, as a heetz?"

The last suggestion speared through my conscious efforts to not think about the female heetz across the way. I flashed on her and me having a nice little dinner of rats we'd caught ourselves, then retiring to a warm little corner somewhere... I stopped that thought in its tracks. I was human, damn it. That's all I wanted to be. Damn the heetz body's programmed instincts. Damn the female heetz for being so enticing to those instincts. And most of all, damn Marilyn for picking this line of conversation. Almost like she knew the kind of effect it was having on me and was enjoying goading me.

I refused to give her any satisfaction. "Can't say I have," I said, hiding any outward sign of the lie by biting into the sandwich.

"I have. The possibilities are endless. Couple centuries from now, they might even have enthak biodroids that are suitable for human nervous systems. Love to get inside one of those. Tentacles, man... tentacles."

"This is all pretty big talk from someone in a human biodroid."

She chuckled. "You know what, Jack? I own this body. Free and clear. The money I make on this job is going to buy me a second biodroid. Right now, I'm leaning towards dolphin. Might change my mind after the tour–maybe go for something a little exotic."

"Or decide to stay with what you've got."

"Doubt it. I imagine three decades of doing the indestructible human routine will be quite enough."

"Still, the way you talk I'd have thought your first time out would have been a little more adventurous."

"Jack," she said, "you think I was born a woman?"

As part of my job, I was given access to every cabin, every crawl space, every crevice on the ship, even those only a few of the highest-ranked officers had access to. That included the shuttle bay. Not many rats in the shuttle bay–it was vented to vacuum often enough for the smarter rats to avoid it, and to teach the dumber ones a final lesson or two. I spent hours in the shuttle bay, most of that time aboard one of the shuttles, where the ship's surveillance system didn't reach, napping in an empty storage locker and dreaming of frolicking on earth in a human body.

A few shifts after the conversation with Marilyn, I was still bothered by her suggestions about me getting together with the female heetz, mostly because of what I'd been feeling in the heetz's presence–feelings of odd, disgusting, alien lust my subconscious kept popping into my mind at the behest of the biodroid programming. Wanting to hunt rats like a heetz was one thing, something I wanted to avoid but could probably live with if I accidentally gave in, but doing it with an alien pet, how could I live with that?

A lot of my shuttle bay time was now devoted to trying to figure out a way to shut the programmed instincts off. Wasn't having much luck. The biodroid didn't have an off switch for them. Not one that I could find, and I'd spent hours combing every inch of my body. Okay, I was actually just grooming myself, but I kept an eye out while I did.

I needed to find an off-switch because I wasn't extremely confident about being able to avoid the instincts with willpower alone. I've never been a strong-willed man. Few men in my family have been. My strongest memory of childhood is of my Dad's futile pay-per-view boycott, and him caving in after three days of sitting in the massage chair watching free TV. Writhing, nervous, chain-smoking as he surfed, all the good channels–the shows he actually paid attention to–blacked out for lack of a credit chip in the set-top box. Huge black gaps between fifty year old sitcoms and colorized reruns of morning game shows. On that third day, in the middle of the afternoon after he'd been surfing for nine hours, flipping continuously every half-second, he went a little nuts. Never saw him move that fast before or since. The way he ravaged Mom's purse looking for a credit chip gave me bad dreams for months to follow.

I didn't want to end up like that, throwing my dignity to the wind, but the longer I spent in the biodroid, the less chance I saw of avoiding the day I would. The instincts were just so strong.

To escape such cheery thoughts crowding my mind, I let myself drift off to sleep, curled up in a shuttle storage locker, the white-noise hum of the air-conditioning unit reassuringly purring at me, like a heetz mother singing to her children. I was dead-to-the-world in seconds.

A much too short time later, I was awakened when the locker ceiling started slamming in to my head. Shuttles don't have their own gravity, and they never shut the gravity off in the big ship, so I had to assume I was being thrown around the locker because the shuttle was under flight.

It's amazing how little attention people pay to their pets. They're always underfoot and after a while become part of the furniture, as long as they don't make a lot of noise. So when I let myself out of the locker and made my way down the aisle to an empty passenger seat, not one of the dozen enthak passengers gave me a second glance.

While I was squirming in the seat to get comfortable, the roof of the shuttle went transparent. An unfamiliar planet hung over us, a gas giant. All reds and yellows. Behind us and out of sight was home-sweet-home, the *Lkit*. Ahead of us, what we were heading towards, was a ship of a very different caliber.

The *Lkit* was big and ugly. Functional. I'd expected any other serious deep space vessel would follow the same design criteria. But that assumption--like ninety-percent of the ones I make--turned out to be very wrong.

According to the readout on the back of the seat in front of me, which was displaying a ton of the kind of trivia geeks and military buffs get boners about, she was a filinav ship called the *Fafofan's Delight*. Only a mile at its widest--physically dwarfed by the *Lkit* yet it looked ten-times larger. Impressive down to my artificial marrow. Awe, they call that. Why it inspired such feelings was the way it changed shape, every so subtly, as we got closer.

When I first began watching it, the filanav ship was shaped like a slightly elongated football. One end glowed ultraviolet--my heetz eyes seeing the glow where my old human eyes would have seen only the yellow-grayish skin of the ship. From the other end came a column of blue-white light, bright enough that the blind could see it, like a welding flame drawn out hundreds of kilometers. The column didn't remain intact. At its terminus, it spread, diffused, became almost a black light, took on the characteristics that marked it for what it was, the ethereal walls of a hyperluminal tube.

As we thrust closer, the column of light snapped off, leaving an afterimage playing in my vision. No longer busy at its task of constructing the hyperluminal tubeway, the ship didn't need to have that particular football shape. Now it needed to accommodate the docking of our shuttle and a different shape was called for. Form follows function, as they say.

Fafofan's Delight began to contract into a more spherical shape. As it did, a bump formed on the surface of the ship. The bump moved, sliding up the sphere until it was directly in front of us. Then the bump became a stalk, reaching out for us, a hollow indent appearing in its end. A shuttle-shaped hollow.

The enthaks in the cabin with me took the whole thing in stride, shutting down lapdecks and checking their uniforms for lint. Doubt they felt the uneasiness I did as the stalk swallowed the shuttle and turned itself inside out.

I got the vague impression of being a piece of food being gently eased down a throat. The ceiling was dark, covered by the material of the stalk as it pushed us along.

Then the sense of movement ended with a slight bump I could feel through the floor of the shuttle. When the stalk withdrew, I saw through the ceiling that the shuttle was now in a large gray-walled room with a domed ceiling. Hangar bay, built to order.

The hatch behind me cycled open. One at a time, the enthaks stretched out to their "standing" shapes and started disembarking. And wouldn't you know, Nu Nu Ia was on board. Wish I had spotted him earlier–I could have high-tailed it back in to the closet instead of sitting around in the open just asking to be caught.

"You," Nu Nu Ia said, finally noticing my presence as he went past. "What are you doing here?"

"Chasing rats," I said, instantly regretting it. "Sir," I added quickly. I wagged my tail in an effort to appear innocent.

Nu Nu Ia looked at me, then the hatch, then me again. "We will discuss this later. For now, stay quiet, and keep close to me."

He spun around and ducked out the hatch. I stood stunned for a second, then followed. Outside the shuttle, the enthaks had formed up into a single-file line and were moving across the hangar, the way their tentacle clusters were fluctuating making them look like they were floating, like nuns on parade. I joined the line, at the end, half-hopping to keep up.

The hangar bay was a few hundred meters wide. At the far end opposite the shuttle the floor was water. The water was tinged slightly green, and smelled like mosquitoes would find a happy home around it. Our little procession stopped about thirty feet from the edge and arranged itself in order of rank into a receiving line, Admiral Yiu Yi Oth on one end, Nu Nu Ia and me at the other.

I was about to scratch myself when the lights dimmed. Nu Nu Ia waived a warning tentacle at me, then pointed at the water.

A dark shape moved through the water. A large head, covered in dark fur, with two oval, dead black eyes on either side of a nasty looking beak, broke the surface and glanced around. Then the rest of the body followed as it worked itself out of the water, using powerful flippers to pull itself up and over the pool's edge. It moved with some amount of grace, surprising, since it had to mass a half-ton or more.

It was the first time I'd seen a filanav in the flesh. It reminded me of a walrus mated with a bull elephant, with a little ostrich thrown in for good measure. Besides its bulk, the only thing that to my mind marked it as alien was its tail, which was long, and at the tip it looked like the fin had evolved joints, effectively becoming a three-digit hand.

The filanav shook itself dry. Some of the water splashed at my feet. The floor swallowed the droplets.

Filanav and enthak stood silent for a moment, then at a slight nod from the filanav, Admiral Yiu Yi Oth stepped forward. He pulled a datacard from a vest pocket and presented it to the filanav with a deep bow. The filanav took the card in its tail hand and held it close to its right eye. Laser light from an implant below its eye scanned the card.

"I suppose you want my blessing on this?" the filanav croaked, my real-time internal translator kicking in automatically.

"Our journey will expand the reach of the Great Filanav Empire." Admiral Yui Yu Oth beamed with pride and self-infatuation, his facial tentacles quivering.

"It will expand your own petty concerns."

"For the glory of the Empire. Always for that."

"Ah, yes," the filanav said, turning towards us. He looked past, then away. "Amazing that you are willing to risk life and limb to explore new worlds, as long as someone else pays the bill."

"I see this as a partnership."

"A partnership? How easily your species believes in its own importance. We build the hyperluminal tubes. We send the real deep space ships out. We make first contact. You simply do the dirty work—the domestication. Never forget that."

"I could sooner forget my children's names," the Admiral said, with no trace of sarcasm in his voice.

"We have given you advantages, major advantages." The filanav put all of its massive weight onto one fore flipper. "There are species that would strip their homeworlds of atmosphere to be in the position we have placed the enthak."

Admiral Yiu Yi Oth bent even deeper into the proper position of respect. "We realize that, Sir."

"Do you?" The filanav brought his beak to bear, inches from the Admiral. Got to give the Admiral credit—he didn't bat an eye flap, despite the smell. From where I was standing, peeking out from behind Nu Nu Ia's tentacle stalk, the filanav's breath made an impression, a smell like sulfur and the fake butter they drown movie theater popcorn in. It couldn't have been pleasant to be beak to nose with the thing.

"Yes, yes we do," Admiral Yi said.

The filanav huffed. "I doubt that, I doubt that. We should be enjoying the fruits of our technology, swimming in the warmest and most beautiful oceans of the worlds of our empire, bearing many happy children, but instead, we find ourselves entrapped in a bureaucracy, slaving at the minutiae of administration, of keeping the tunnels open, of fending off pirates and lesser species with expansionist ideas. And all the while, you flit from world to world ignorant of the resources that allow your flight. I ask you, is that fair?"

"Not from that perspective, no."

"Then it is a good thing we receive pleasure from merely providing you with opportunities–that our emotional well-being does not depend on seeing our wards achieve results."

The Admiral made to protest, "Sir..."

The filanav's long tail whipped around with the speed of a whip. The long fingers on the tip of the tail were open, and they struck the Admiral's neck and head like a cat-of-nine-tails. The Admiral reeled, but didn't fall. His tentacles were spread out enough to let him maintain his balance.

The filanav didn't wait for the Admiral to recover his composure. "What do you bring to us in exchange for our magnanimousness? More worlds to hold sway over, more beings to administrate, to be responsible for. Where is the true glory, the truly valuable?"

"Give this journey a chance, and we may please you yet."

For a moment the filanav looked like it was going to hit the Admiral again. Instead, it lumbered to the edge of the pool.

"I doubt that, I doubt that."

It dove into the water, and was soon lost from sight in the depths.

The ride back to the *Lkit* was pure torture, in the literal, psychological sense of the concept.

I sensed a certain tension in the air as we boarded, more smelled it than anything else. enthak emote via fragrance sometimes. Not a bad smell altogether, sort of like cherries in butter, but it worried me. A sense of foreboding settled over me as I waited for everyone to take their seats. Instead of taking a seat myself, I headed for the storage locker, hoping to spend the trip nicely isolated inside it, but Nu Nu Ia slapped a tentacle across the door when I tried to open it, preventing me from reaching safe haven.

"A word with you," Nu Nu Ia said, tilting his head at a nearby chair. "About your service record."

"I thought we had that all settled," I said, hoping to avoid what I suspected was coming. Instead of opening lapdecks or chatting with each other, every enthak in the cabin was looking sternly, silently, in my direction.

"So had I," Nu Nu Ia said, guiding me towards the seat. Shoving me. "Until I found you aboard this shuttle, instead of doing your job."

A wave of muttered disapprovals swept through the officers. I was about to say something when Admiral Yiu Yu Oth himself spoke up. "This is the one you mentioned at the staff briefing yesterday, Ia? The rat-catcher that doesn't catch rats?"

"The same."

The shuttle was gently being lifted toward the hangar ceiling. Admiral Yiu Yu Oth shuffled his tentacles, looked around the cabin at the other officers. Those that met his gaze seemed to know what he was thinking. "Now would be an opportune time for an impromptu service review, then, wouldn't it?"

Nu Nu Ia remained standing behind me, keeping a tentacle on my shoulder. "Yes, yes it would, Admiral."

The Admiral looked in my direction. "Good. I will begin by explaining to you, rat-catcher, exactly what level of performance I expect from all members of my crew–and what is done to those who do not meet my expectations."

The way Nu Nu Ia had shoved me into the seat, forcing me to sit on my own tail. Hurt like hell, all bent the wrong way. I tried shifting it out from under me, but Nu Nu Ia pushed down hard on my shoulder to keep me sitting exactly like I was.

At least it wouldn't last long, I thought. Ten minutes, at most, and we'd be docked back on the *Lkit*. I could take the pain, and the coming verbal abuse, for ten minutes. No problem.

"Nu, please inform the shuttle pilot AI to postpone landing and circle the *Lkit* until we are through here." The Admiral slowly rubbed the side of his head where the filanav had shown him who was boss. "And have another shuttle standing by to refuel us. This could take some time."

The ten minutes lasted seven grueling hours. Grueling for me–the enthaks had a good old time. They were all happy and genial with each other when we finally docked and disembarked, making small talk about the upcoming mission, enthusiastic again, the whole bit about the Admiral being slapped around forgotten, or at the least, suppressed.

Me, I left the shuttle bay in pain.

A great deal of the pain was mental, from the almost clinical way my work record had been examined, critiqued, insulted, denigrated, you name it, to the point where it became obvious that regardless of the facts, they were determined to make me out as the absolute worst rat-catcher ever to serve on any enthak ship-of-the-line.

But that's not to say some of the pain wasn't physical, mind you. I had a good number of welts on my chest and thighs where the officers, in a merry round-robin session allegedly intended to inspire loyalty and obedience, had taken jabbing pokes at me. And my tail wouldn't unbend right after all that sitting on it. I'd have to track down a ship's mechanic to have it looked at.

No time for that then, though, since to reinforce the lessons, I was being forced to work the next three shifts straight, with no break. For my own well-being, the Admiral said. Give me a chance to prove myself.

The whole thing had left me disenchanted. And angry. Prowling the vents and ducts of the ship, limping a little thanks to the bend in my tail, I couldn't help but let my anger at the enthak boil into a good seething rage. They had a lot of nerve treating me like that just to compensate for their own feelings of inadequacy and shame. The bastards. How dare they! Didn't they know I was dealing with my own problems?

My seethe was interrupted by the patter of rat feet. There it was, crawling low along the metal-grating floor, a meffi. And damned if it didn't have a tyrpe in its mouth. Up ahead, just around a bend of tubing, was one of my traps. Obviously, the meffi had plans for the tyrpe.

I reached for the dart gun holster under my lower left arm. Its darts were filled with a real nasty nerve poison, guaranteed to make anything it struck dance in pain for a while before it killed them. The safety strap clicked when I undid it.

The meffi heard me. It stopped, stared at me for a few seconds, and then continued towards the trap. Contempt, that's what I saw in its little beady eyes. I was no more a threat to it than the dead tyrpe it carried in its mouth.

That, more than everything, pissed me off. Big time.

Everything snapped into clarity right then. It was the moment I had dreaded, worried over for months, ever since I'd found myself in a heetz in the hospital, and now that it was here, I wondered why I'd been dreading it so much. I knew how Dad must have felt scrambling for the pay-per-view box, credit chip in hand. A sublime sense of relief settled over me. It felt right, and it wasn't just the biodroid talking.

It was time to take Marilyn's advice and use my biodroid for all it was worth, and to hell with my misplaced sense of self-dignity. Like she'd said, I'd have eternity to find it again—if I even needed it. The ethnak certainly did fine without their own dignity.

I dropped the gun, and leapt. Landing easily on all sixes. The meffi must have realized the rules had changed. It shrieked, dropping the tyrpe, and darted up the crawl space. The smell of its trail flared in my nostrils like a beacon. I let the wall between my conscious mind and the biodroid's subsystems crumble. I tore after the meffi, the trail singing to me.

The meffi was fast, but I was just as fast. And it made the mistake of running down a vent that dead-ended in a grate.

Dinner time.

I trotted up to the mess hall, feeling good about catching the meffi, and only a little guilty about giving in to the biodroid instincts. That guilt would fade. There'd be plenty of time to see to that.

Marilyn was there, of course, drinking. And so, as I had hoped, was the female heetz.

Marilyn would help me get drunk enough to do what I knew had to be done next. The heetz, she was what had to be done next.

I caught the heetz's eye. Rolled back on my heels. She did the same and my inner thighs tingled.

I'm pretty certain Dad wouldn't be proud, but I think he'd understand.

Two

AMERICAN SUICIDAL

FRIDAY, 9:59 PM PACIFIC. The center of the universe. Hollywood.

This is how Jack Brasca gets himself laid, week-in, week-out. At least during the season.

Jack's sitting in a horseshoe booth at the back of this dive of a nightclub in Century City, his regular place, sandwiched between club-trawling wannabe starlets lured to the table by Jack's buddy Donny, the club owner, with the promise of free drinks. Their attention's not on Jack–fat and bearded, dressed like a bum, not even trying in a town where trying is really all there is. No, they're watching the big flat over the bar. Exactly where he wants their attention anyway.

The latest episode of one of the most watched shows in the world is starting its weekly premier stream. Every flat in the nightclub is tuned in. The DJ's stopped the jams, conversations have faded to whispers.

The theme-dirge signature chord strikes.

American Suicide.

Where people tell their life stories and then at the close of the show end it all while the world watches. Tastefully, sitting on an unadorned stage, sometimes surrounded by loved-ones. They swallow a pill calculated to their body weight to kill them clean and painless in one and a half minutes. Long enough for final words and a slow camera push in to their slacking face while the music swells.

Formulaic, but it works. And works well.

Before the credits, a preview of the evening's episode. A forty-one year old childless divorcee from Columbus with a serious riverboat casino addiction. Her "appearance" fee will pay off her gambling debt, post mortem.

"Keep your eyes on the screens, girls," Donny says, coming back to the table right on cue. He slips onto the end of the seat, thumbs up at the bar flat, the show credits flashing over a montage of smiling, soft focus faces serene in their last minutes.

Created by Jack Brasca.

"That's my boy, here," Donny says. "Told you girls he was somebody."

That gets a smile back at him from the redhead, the kind you might give a puppy the first time he figures out how to avoid pissing on your shoe. These girls know the business, know exactly what the credit means. Means if he's here, in this place, looking like he does, he's probably washed up, surviving on the royalty from getting lucky once, pitching an idea somebody else turned into gold.

Donny clears his throat. Everyone looks up at the flat.

Executive Producer Jack Brasca.

That gets them all smiling back at him, lust in their eyes: He's no wash-out, he's a living, breathing show-runner. He can do things for their careers. And for that, they are willing to do things to him.

And he intends to give them every opportunity.

"Well," Jack says, like he says every week, "guess I should buy another round, then?"

The redhead scoots in closer to him. Jack nods thanks at Donny, snaps his fingers for the waiter. He slips his other hand up under the redhead's leather mini.

His chest pulses a samba. Denise calling.

She knows better than to call him during the show, his celebratory downtime after a week's hard work. He ignores it. He'll listen to the voicemail later. Maybe tomorrow morning. Give the redhead a little thrill calling the office from bed.

The samba stops and Jack leans in to whisper a suggestion to the redhead that they leave for a real party. And maybe pick out one of the other girls to come along with them.

Samba starts up again almost immediately. Denise must have hung up before voice mail and called again. Which means she has to talk to him. Now.

Jack sighs, reluctantly withdraws his hand from the redhead's panties and pulls his phone out. "What?"

"You watching the numbers?"

"The whole point of having an executive production assistant is I don't have to do much actual work, Denise.–What about the numbers?"

He asks, but he knows. They're lifeblood. The streaming numbers. People and bots, real-time world-wide, clicking in to watch the show during its premiere stream. The initial indication of a show's eventual total viewership.

"They're off," Denise says, her voice cracking a bit the way it does when she's excited. Or nervous. "--Down a full percent from last week."

"Show just started. It'll pick up."

"It's trending down, Jack."

"Wouldn't worry about it. Third game of the NBA finals started an hour ago. We'll make it up on downloads. Always do."

"Don't think so. We're losing teen and tween girls, not core."

Tweens don't watch basketball. Jack reaches for his gin and tonic. "Time-shifting?"

"Prelims say downloads are gonna get hit, too."

Downloads are where the real money is. Thing is, they're usually automated, set and forget. If they're down, could be tech problems somewhere out in the cloud. Or could be people are making a pre-determined, conscious–unforgivable–choice. "What's doing it? Chile net segment go down again?" he asks optimistically.

"First thing I checked. Total net audiences are normal. Up a little over average, even. Something's pulling our audience."

He's mulling that over as movement up at the bar gets his attention. Somebody's talking to the bartender, pointing at the big flat, the first segment of *Suicide* playing out, the back-story, telling the degenerate gambler divorcee's sad tale. The bartender shrugs, grabs the remote and does the unthinkable.

He changes the stream. The fucker. Jack shoots a concerned glance at Donny who just shrugs back at him, already drunk and paying attention to the girls, not the flats.

The new stream is some dark and grainy video. Not even super-hi-d. Foreign language narration–is that Russian?–over a gothic castle.

The show's title pops up in Cyrillic and English and Jack's stomach instinctively sinks.

Final Exit.

"Jack, you there?"

Soon every flat in the place is switching over and people are gathering under them. The girls in the booth get restless, wonder what all the fuss is about.

"I'm coming in," Jack says into the phone. "I'm gonna want the entire team there."

"Crew, too?"

"Yeah." He jabs the phone off and it rings again almost instantly. Not a samba. Flight of the Bumblebees. The studio. VP of Programming Robert Ikita's private line. What a surprise he's watching the numbers, too.

Jack takes a deep breath, answers. "Bob, hey. I'm just checking it now. I'll get back to you."

He hangs up before Ikita can object, say anything at all.

Donny's standing to let the girls out. "What's up, Jack?"

Jack stuffs his phone away, his lips in a thoughtful smile. "Competition, is all. I might have to actually do some work this week. --Doggie bag me up a pitcher of gin and tonics for the road, can ya?"

One AM, Saturday morning. Jack back at the studio, in his office watching the Russian suicide knock-off show for a fourth time with Denise and *Suicide*'s director, Nora.

On the wall flat, a fragile, wheelchair-bound ballerina with terminal leukemia is twirled around the grand ballroom of a Balkan castle by her partner/lover, both of them sluggish and slowing. Dying from the poison they've downed as part of the routine. Struggling to complete the dance. Narration in Russian, the subtitles off, only the overlay of quickly fading vitals at the bottom of the screen.

"They're not very good dancers," Nora notes from the couch in the corner.

Jack shrugs. "She's in a wheelchair, he's killing himself for her, probably a little stressed. What you expect?"

The guy stumbles out of a simple pirouette, a first miss-step. The girl reaches out for him, panic in her eyes. The guy recovers, but now it's the girl who's slumping, unable to keep her head up. No recovering this time. The poison setting in, the guy's knees go out, just buckle. He collapses at her feet, neck twisted unnaturally to look up at her. She struggles to reach down to him, touch him one last time, but inertia's sending her chair in the wrong direction, and she dies, rolling away.

Vitals flatline. Soaring music, fade to black and Cyrillic credits. Jack touches his desk and the flat switches over to silent world headline aggregate mode. There among the wars and economic meltdowns, just as he expected, is a slug about *American Suicide*: "Russian Challenger Euthanizes *Suicide*"

Jack snorts. "Yeah, well that's clever."

It's the most-read story.

"Seriously," Nora says. "I did five years hard labor dance class when I was a kid and I know from bad ballet. They're definitely not pros."

The new intern, the one with the bob haircut and the nice legs–Steph, or something, he thinks–comes in with a second tray of coffees and donuts. Smiles at Jack in that way interns who want to become more than interns do while she's setting the tray in front of him. He gives her a polite thank-you leer and she leaves. He grabs a coffee, makes a mental note to explore career opportunities with her. Later.

"Doesn't matter," he says. "They are pros for the sake of ten minutes screen time. Makes a better story. Her promising career cut short by disease. Him, perfectly healthy with an equally promising career, giving it up for the sake of their love. Takes it right into tragedy. Hell, for all we know, she isn't even sick. Pretty fuckin' brilliant."

"A little unethical, isn't it?" Nora asks.

"We give people an international stage to kill themselves," Denise notes, plucking up a donut.

"Okay, yeah," Nora says. "But we're not dishonest about it. We let their story stand on its own, warts and all. People expect that from us."

"And maybe that's exactly why we're losing to the Russians." Jack asks. "People know what they'll get from us, what they've gotten for two years–so why bother ordering us up? People get bored. The Russians have novelty going for them–and they maybe aren't letting the facts get in the way of telling a better story. A tragic love story, dramatized through a fuckin' dance, for Christ's sake. Not some poor slob sitting on a bare stage downing a pill, week after week."

"So, we tweak our presentation. Maybe a new set?"

Jack shakes his head. "This is gonna take more than a new set, Nora. We have to get outside our comfort zone."

"You want to go violent?" Nora's face scrunches with distaste. They've had this discussion before. "That's a mistake."

"We have to shore up core audience numbers." Adult 30 to 55. The ones that tell focus groups they watch for the pathos but really watch to see somebody only slightly more desperate than themselves give up and die. "Russians screwed up, only hit us on story. Missed a chance to erode us on two fronts. If they go violent, we're really screwed. We have to pre-emptive strike."

"The studio'll never let us," Nora balks. "The Catholic League's always looking for a chance to sue us again. And it's an election year."

"I've already talked to Ikita," Jack says. "Studio's signed off."

And so much for that. Nora slumps back into the couch.

"How?" Denise asks. "I wouldn't even know where to start... Who to bring in. We'd have to bring somebody in, right?"

"I got it handled." Jack reaches for a drawer, pulls out this tiny, intricate clockwork device—cogs and armatures encaging a three-inch kids cartoon action figure, spray-painted gold. He sits it on the desk and sets it ticking. "I've been getting these little things every month for a year now. Calling cards from some outfit that wants a shot at being our suicide go-to guys. Don't think they actually watch the show, but they're pretty ingenious."

A bell goes off inside the device and the thing lets off a puff of steam. A miniature garden shears pops out, snips the doll's head in half.

Smirking, Jack picks up the plastic skull top. Clean cut. "I'll call it a try-out. Get the first one free. And at the very least put 'em on retainer so the Russians can't snag 'em."

Nora shrugs. "That keeps the core audience watching—and add a whole new sicko demo to our viewership, no doubt. But what about the kids? The girls?"

When all was said and done, the numbers there were down a full three and a half percent over last week. A small percentage, but it translated into huge real audience numbers—and more importantly, huge real advertising and downstream revenue lost.

"The damage is done for this week," Jack says. "The trick is getting them back next week. A lot of them are just gonna stick with the Russians, and after a whole week of school buzz, they're gonna bring their friends. Gonna be a tidal wave."

"How do we stop the wave?" Denise asks.

"Give them a better story," Jack says. He jogs his head at a stack of manila folders on his desk in front of Denise. "That the latest batch of loser applicants?"

"The vetted ones, yeah." Denise pushes the stack at him. "Not much to work with in here, though. Springtime, everybody gets optimistic about their lives."

Jack flips open the top folder, scans it. Recent widower, in his fifties, misses his dearly departed. Under normal circumstances, it'd do, but this time, two seconds and Jack knows it's not what he needs. He tosses it aside, opens the next one. "Leave that to me."

"We can't just make shit up," Nora says.

"Russians don't seem to have a problem with it," Jack says. Discard, open. The stack's getting shorter. "And apparently audiences don't care."

"There *are* regulations. Just because they haven't hauled us to D.C. to testify lately doesn't mean Congress isn't watching."

Discard, open. "We can tweak."

"Manipulate," Nora says.

"Embellish for dramatic effect." Jack looks up into Nora's disapproving glare. "Gotta give the kids something."

Even if we have to make it up from whole cloth, he thinks, opening the last folder. Sean Reed. He'll have to do.

"Your mother's terminal?"

Monday morning. Jack sits in the interview room across a small table from Sean Reed. Late thirties, comb over, bulbous. Dressed like a software engineer: white shirt, striped tie, khakis with too many pockets. Total lump.

"Without the life support, yes," Reed says.

"Car accident, right?" Jack scans Reed's application, folder open on his lap. Nine months ago Reed was driving his mother home after dinner and lost control of the car, took a header straight into a tree. Reed was wearing a belt, his mother wasn't. In the file, there's a yellow stick-on note from one of the shrinks who interviewed Reed during the exhaustive application vetting process. Strong suspicions that Reed hadn't *lost* control at all.

"I'd had some wine," Reed says. He drips guilt. His hands would be trembling if they weren't wrapped around an *American Suicide* logo mug. "Only a glass, but my night vision's not that great to begin with."

"Astigmatism, myself," Jack says. "Okay. Tell me why you want to do this?"

Reed stares into the mug. "I've been laid off. Could barely afford the expenses before, but now... I don't have any choice."

"But your mother never wanted to be kept alive by artificial means anyway, right?"

"We'd discussed it—she didn't want people making a fuss. Time's up, it's up, she always said, just pissing God off by sticking around unwelcome."

"So, gotta ask, why'd you keep her alive this long?"

Reed's eyes flick up to glare at Jack. "She's my mother... all I have. I couldn't..."

"I understand. Had to ask. How about power of attorney?" Jack twists to ask Foster, *Suicide*'s staff attorney, sitting at the end of the table behind a closed attaché case and a tripod-mounted vidcam recording the conversation for the inevitable lawsuit. Sometimes more than one.

"Is Mr. Reed's, yes," Foster says. "Everything's in order."

"Super." Jack turns back to Reed. "Still, doesn't mean you have to take your own life."

"I can't live without her," Reed says. Which Jack reads as: Can't live with what I did. Nothing else to live for, either.

Yeah, total lump. But the story's solid. Loser momma's boy wants to kill himself for leaving his mother a vegetable, accident or not, and better yet, wants to pull the plug on mom, first, right there with him on stage.

Not the doomed-ballerinas-in-love-level tragedy they need to beat the Russians, not much of a tragedy at all, just another sad-luck story with an interesting twist, but Jack sees potential in it as a start. All he has to do is add that something more. Something Nora will object to, no doubt, but it's his show, and he's not about to lose it out of a naïve loyalty to facts. When has entertainment ever been about facts?

Now all Jack has to do is figure out what the something more is. No problem, he chuckles grimly to himself. He's got a whole four days.

"I think we can help you, Mr. Reed."

Reed swallows. The guilt-driven ones always do. They're not killing themselves because deep down they want to. They're doing it because they believe they have to. To make right whatever they did wrong. But there's always a part of them, even deeper down–the survival part–that believes they'll be just as forgiven if they make the gesture honestly but are turned down, no fault of their own. They tried–the universe doesn't want them to kill themselves.

Guys like Reed, a little counseling, even just a friend to have a few beers with, they'd learn to live with the guilt. But Jack's got a show to run. "It's not fair, to her, living like this, asking you to live like this, but no one would blame you, you get up and walk away right now. The pain will fade. Eventually."

Reed stares into his mug. "The money will go to some kind of memorial for her?"

"We'll take care of that. Something nice... maybe a tree. With a brass plaque."

"She'd like that," Reed says, nodding, and he's sold. "How's it work?"

"Paperwork, first," Jack says, leaning back with a slight smile. "There's always paperwork. Believe it or not, that's the hardest part. Foster will walk you through it."

Foster opens her attaché, starts laying out thick stacks of contract and a pen while Jack presses on. "After that's all done with, you'll leave here today with a camera crew. They'll follow you, document the next couple days as you go about settling your affairs, telling your story, visiting your mother in the hospital, going about your normal end of life. We'll edit those down into the first two segments."

"Okay," Reed says, distracted as Foster starts leafing through the contract, explaining what each release commits him to, showing him where to sign. Intentionally talking at the same time as Jack.

"By Thursday," Jack continues, "my team will have worked out the mechanics of the suicides, so you'll come in and we'll do a dry-run. Practice, just to make sure everything works."

Reed looks up from scribbling his name. "I have to practice taking a pill?"

"We were thinking about going in a slightly different direction this time. If you're up for something special."

"As long as it doesn't hurt," Reed says, shrugging, signing another paper.

"You have my word."

The conference room door opens. Steph the intern, here to freshen their coffees.

Jack catches Reed stealing a glance at her ass, then guiltily turning his attention back to the contract. Busily, dutifully signing.

———————————

"So I'm thinking we put the mother here."

Monday afternoon. Jack's on the stage, standing under dead spotlights.

"Yeah, sure. Coma Mom here." Portland, self-described performance machine artiste, traces the outline of a hospital bed with the needle-tip of his boot. Not a centimeter of his skin without some sort of shiny squiggle of a chromatic tattoo. A silver chain runs from eyebrow to earlobe to bottom lip to collar bone. His t-shirt tells Jack to fuck off in seventeen languages. "We gonna need to build a bed, too?"

"The hospital will send her over in one," Jack says.

"You sure?" Denver, the other half of Team Weight State. The marginally business half. Fewer tats, no visible piercings, purple velvet tux. "Custom bed, we could really do something up nice."

"Something?" Jack asks.

Portland shrugs. "Like we could rig the bed to shake her, make her thrash."

"Shit," Denver says, getting excited, "we could make her sit up and scream like a banshee with her final breath, if ya want. Or twist her head around all Linda Blair, throw pea-soup over the guy."

"Let's keep the focus on the son, okay?" Jack begins to doubt his decision to give these guys a chance, even pro-bono. "So, how does the son pull the plug on her?"

"Simple thumb-switch plunger on this baby, right under his hand and cabled to her life support system." Portland pats one of the arms of the hulking device Jack's been purposefully ignoring, the one they'd brought, spent the morning setting up. "He hits the plunger, and once she's flat-lined, that'll start the shavers."

It's seven feet high, a bronze pipe and black rubber tube X-shaped cross on a pedestal, with basketball-sized chrome cylinders at each point of the cross. Wide, weathered leather straps at the right places to keep a man secure, immobile.

"Well," Jack says. "I did say I wanted something special. How's it work?"

"All the fun stuff's in these cylinders here," Portland says, brimming with pride as he flips a latch and opens a panel on a cylinder to reveal intricate piping and gears. "First stage, a spray of misted liquid nitrogen. Contact-freezes the flesh a few dozen millimeters thick. Then these micro-lathes swing in, shave off the top millimeters."

Denver steps behind the device, tugs Jack along. "The cylinders are in constant motion along these tracks. So it's fingers and toes first, then hands and feet, then wrists and ankles. Freeze, shave, move further up the limb, repeat. Nice and smooth..."

Smiling, Portland holds his left hand out to Jack, fingers splayed. His index, middle, and ring fingers are all the same length. Neatly trimmed back a centimeter, squared off half way down the index finger's nail. "Didn't feel a thing."

Jack looks away, embarrassed that he's tasting bile. How many deaths has he seen and this gets to him? He's such a baby sometimes. "Speed?" he asks Denver.

"Variable. Faster you go, the less freezing actually takes place. Less freezing, more pain."

"We'll want slow, for this. Guy can watch his mom die in peace," Jack says, his stomach settling, starting to see the potential here. "What happens when the cylinders finish off the arms and legs? They start boring into the torso?"

"Thought about that," Portland says, closing up the cylinder, "but it gets bloody, and you said you wanted PG-13."

"Trick is you have to shave off everything all at once, not bore," Denver says. "Otherwise you've got stuff around the hole oozing out, the guy in the harness sees it and --"

Portland chuckles. "The pig we tested it on panicked, thrashed itself out of the harness. Had to cut its throat."

Denver's expression turns momentarily gaunt with memory. "We could have put in a drug system to knock out the victim so he's unconscious by then, but the whole point is to let the guy stay aware as long as possible."

"So?" Jack asks.

"So, we got these," Portland says, pointing at a pair of much larger cylinders tucked behind the intersection of the cross beams. "Big enough to shave the torso and head at the same time. When the little ones are finished, these puppies snap up around from the back and start in from the sides. They have to move a little faster, and the guy'll be dead before they're half finished, but the visual of the sides closing in on the head, eyes wide open, darting back and forth... that'll be pretty neat, we think."

"Yeah, yeah, I see it," Jack says, nodding. "But I was thinking we go for a softer last moment. How about instead of the side shavers, there's a vat of acid underneath all this... when the shavers finish with the limbs the harness drops him into it? Slides down. Camera follows the eyes down."

"Could work," Portland says. "Put a weight belt on the guy so the head stays above the acid?"

"Until the very last possible second," Jack says. "Give the cameras time to lock on the eyes through the acid mist."

"Good visual," Denver says.

"What I'm thinking, yeah," Jack says.

Portland's sizing up the rear cylinders, already trying to figure out what he needs to reconfigure it. "Yeah, we can do that."

Jack smiles. "So, you guys ever think about merchandizing?"

Two AM Wednesday morning. Jack in his office, leaned back in his chair, watching the dailies on the wall flat, the camera crew following Reed around. He usually doesn't watch the dailies, but Denise had insisted this time. The prod team's getting worried Reed's story–or Reed himself–might not make for the Russian-topping show Jack's been telling them it will.

The vid cuts to Reed telling his story to an off-screen Denise. Sitting there hunched and defeated, eyes staring blankly out at nothing, voice a monotone.

"Okay, yeah, the guy's a lump," Jack says. "But show me a suicide who isn't."

A lot of the suicides are that way, turned off, ready to die. They jazz it up in editing, add narration to smooth and move things along. Denise is overreacting. The *Final Exit* pressure getting to her, is all, making her question everything.

But she was right about one thing, Jack thinks: The story as it stands isn't gonna beat the Russians. Knew that going in, and Team Weight State's killing cross is only half the battle.

The other half... an idea's been percolating for a day. Maybe it's time to let it boil over.

"Still... maybe we're on the wrong track. The Russians did death conquering love," Jack says. "Old-world depressing Shakespeare tragedy crap. All well and good..." He takes a sip of cold coffee, puts the empty mug down on the desk. "...but all tragedy, all the time? Nah. People want a happy ending every once in a while. We should be giving them love conquering death. Totally off-format, but that's what'll sell it, really make it big. An all-out, all-American Howard Hawks screwball-comedy happy ending. --So, you think you're up for it?"

Steph the intern looks up from between his legs. "I want a producer's credit."

Jack smiles down at her. "Well, naturally."

Friday morning. Ten AM.

Denise is waiting for Jack at the studio door. Pacing, smoking—something she only does when the world is collapsing around them. Or she thinks it is. Which is exactly the state he was hoping to find her in.

"Well, we're in a panic this morning, aren't we?" he asks, barely able to hide his pleased-with-his-own-cleverness smile.

"Have to show you something before they get here," Denise says.

"Before who gets here?" He opens the studio door. The air inside is cool and dark, inviting. "Anyway, whatever it is it had better be bad at least as funny as 1980s porn. Spent yesterday having my asshole widened by the advertisers, could really use the laugh."

Denise flicks her cigarette away, instantly takes out another one as she follows him in. "Serious, Jack."

"My office, then," he says with a chuckle.

In his office, he slips into his chair while Denise fires up the flat, tuning it to the in-house feed from the control room. Paused vid of Reed standing at the craft services table, picking through the spread of bagels and fruit.

"This is from yesterday." Denise taps the desk and the vid starts playing.

"Well, okay, the guy's having a snack. Nervous, yeah, but who isn't on run-through day?"

"Watch."

A brunette in jeans and t-shirt, no bra, nice legs, saunters up to the table, says hi to Reed with a coy smile and flip of the hair. Steph, overplaying it a bit, Jack sees, but Reed's not catching on something's up. Jack's surprised Denise isn't, either.

"Ohh... scandalous," Jack says. "Someone's talking to him."

"Flirting."

"That what that is? So what? She's just being nice to the guy, giving him a little thrill before he dies. Big deal."

Denise lights yet another smoke. "They ended up going to dinner together."

The playback switches to hand-held footage of Reed and Steph at a restaurant, Steph slowly breaking Reed out of his shell over deep-fried squid.

"Man's gotta eat. Interns, too."

"They went back to her place before the entrée."

Steph taking Reed's hand, pulling him up from the table.

"We got vid of that?" Jack asks. "You know, the sex?"

"They asked the crew to stay outside."

"And they actually did?" Jack asks. "Damn it, I told Frank to do what he had to do. The place doesn't have windows? Shit, they could have gotten one of those colon camera things, drilled a hole through the wall and snaked it through... something."

Denise sags. "You knew."

"Knew?" Jack asks, insulted. "Engineered."

"Jesus, Jack... embellishing's one thing, but manufacturing a story?"

"There's no way I'm letting the Russians kill us."

"Nora's gonna shit."

"She's a pragmatist. She'll come 'round once she sees the results."

"If she doesn't walk out before the shoot."

"Town's full of directors."

Denise lets out a long huff and for a second Jack thinks maybe she's thinking about walking off herself. "Just hope you know what you're doing–Reed and Miss Intern are on their way over. Frank called. They stopped to pick up a lawyer first."

"There is a signed contract, Mr. Reed."

Friday. 11 AM. Conference room at the studio. Jack and Foster on one side, Reed, Steph and their new lawyer on the other. Camera crew in the corner, recording everything. Jack had insisted over Foster's objections.

Foster's been doing all the talking so far, Jack silent, letting her, sitting there playing with his tie, flicking a loose thread on the tag.

"A contract to commit suicide," Reed's lawyer says. He's a slick one, with billboards all over LA. Been friends with Jack since high school. Was bemused when Jack called Thursday morning and asked him to play along, anything unusual happened the next couple days, like getting a visit from someone named Steph. "By its very nature, anyone signing it is under severe emotional stress. It could be argued any such contract is automatically void due to temporary incompetence."

"Could be argued," Foster says. "Has been argued. But never successfully. There's a reason we have a screening process, why you can't even apply for the show without a battery of carefully designed psychological evaluations by a highly trained and respected staff. The bottom line, we have precedence... we have obtained judicial compliance orders before."

"Please," Reed says, tearing his eyes away from Steph's and turning directly to Jack. "You can't make me go through with this. I thought I didn't have anything in my life, but now..."

Steph leans in close to Reed. "He's got something to live for."

Reed goes back to staring into Steph's blues. "Yes, yes I do."

Steph turns to Jack but she's playing to the camera. "We'll do what we have to, Jack, to be together. For a long time. Sue us, whatever you have to do, but you can't force Sean to kill himself. It's not right."

Calls him Jack, not Mr. Brasca like they'd rehearsed, like a respectful supplicant begging for her lover's life should. An innocent slip? Or something else? Her way of letting him know a producer's credit isn't the last thing she expects for this?

She's not that subtle, or clever. But still... Jack being who and what he is, he can't take any chances, can he? But he does genuinely feel sorry for her.

"What's right is abiding by a signed contract, for which Mr. Reed's estate has already been paid," Foster says. "Do I have to call a judge, here?"

"No need for phone calls, Meagan," Jack tells Foster, smoothing down his tie. He grins up at a confused Reed. "You'll have to excuse the lawyers–they are by nature and design short-sighted. This is a better story."

"It is?" Foster asks.

Jack nods. "A man so torn up by guilt, loneliness, and hopelessness that he would rather kill himself then face life without the one rock in his life–even though she's a vegetable–but who finds a reason to live and hope and dream again. And better yet, he finds it thanks to the very show he was planning to end it all on. Now, that's a story."

Jack turns to the camera. They're ready for him, already pushing in on his face.

"True love found, and none too soon. Our audience would kill us we didn't let these two have a life together. And I don't think I could honestly live with myself, I stood in their way." Jack waits for the cameraman to point the rig at Reed and Steph, waits a beat to make sure their giddy embrace is caught in focus. "--Now, you love-birds get out of here, I've got a show to completely rethink at the last minute."

Five PM Friday. Control room.

"This is never gonna top the Russians," Nora says, settling down into her chair in front of a vast curving bank of flats and boards.

Jack's standing behind her, looking down at the stage through the control room window. A mid-fifties woman in a coma lies on a hospital bed, a rack of life support equipment behind her. A single spotlight illuminates her peaceful, machine-controlled breathing. A fragile chest rises and falls under white cotton blankets and tubing. Team Weight State's killing cross is nowhere to be seen, no need for it now.

"It's a love story," Jack says. "Kids love the love stories."

Jack's a little surprised Nora's talking to him. When he told her about the complication, the new direction for the night's show, she'd just left his office without saying a word. Pretty obvious she knows he set up the whole thing. But she's a sucker for a happy ending, he guesses, willing to let him create this one, even with her doubts.

Going to be a trick keeping her from quitting when it really goes down. Of all of this, it's that he's actually nervous about. He jokes, but the show wouldn't be the same without her.

"We're gonna lose core," she says over her shoulder, surveying the flats.

"Core will have plenty to chew on, trust me."

Nora arches an eyebrow at him as she issues a flurry of curt commands. Her team slips into well-oiled action.

The main monitor flat fades up on the bed, Reed's mother. Holds a few seconds for narration and music to be added later. A finger snap from Nora and the camera pans to the side of the stage. Where Howie, *Suicide*'s on-air host, is escorting Reed and Steph out onto the stage.

Reed looks nervous, uncertain, first time seeing his mother laying there awaiting her fate, oblivious. Steph at his side, clenching his hand, helps him along. Almost tugging him as Howie herds them towards the bed. Anxious to get this over with, get her credit and whatever else she can get from Jack.

Howie says a few words at the edge of the bed, suggests Reed take a moment to say goodbye and press the small button welded onto the bed rail when he's ready, then recedes into the shadows, leaving the pair alone with Reed's mother.

Reed looks down into his mother's face, tries to talk, say something. Mouth moves, no words. He looks away.

Nora snaps her fingers and a camera pushes in tight to Reed's hesitant, guilt-torn face, Steph leaning in close. "It'll be okay, honey. She'll understand. You've got me, now..."

Reed works his lower lip, manages a slight nod.

And then Steph's guiding Reed's reluctant hand to the button. Helping him press it, her hand over his.

The stage lights dim to accentuate the spotlight on Reed's mother and the life support equipment, the compressor deflating. Indicators fluctuate and trail to flatline.

A shotgun mike picks up the small sound of a choking gag. Her chest heaves with a last peaceful breath.

The camera pulls back to catch Reed's tears. He's turning to nestle his head in Steph's shoulder when the rumbling starts.

The woman convulses, her hips bucking under the covers. A moment of violent shaking and her torso springs up.

The old woman sits there, a dead face, mouth gaping open, head lolled loose to one side.

The only person in the control room that's surprised is Nora. Jack had briefed everybody else to expect something, be ready if Nora loses it. She swivels around to glare at him. He's about to call out for her assistant director to take over when a raspy, old-woman voice bellows from down on the stage, gets Nora to turn and look.

"You... promised..."

Jack steps up close behind Nora, leans down. "Wide shot," he suggests in a whisper.

"Fuck you," she says. But she snaps her fingers twice just in time to catch the robotic arms emerging from underneath the bed, steel talon-tipped brass claws outstretched, reaching out for Reed and encircling him.

The lump doesn't resist. Jack swears he looks relieved.

The robot arms lift Reed up, pull him down on top of the corpse, a final embrace.

The arms tighten and Reed lets out a scream of pain, crushed against his dead mother and the reinforced bed.

The shotgun mike picks up his spine snapping.

Steph's need to scream finally overcomes her shock, then. Jack feels a small tinge of guilt for not telling her all of the details of his little plan. But that's all he feels guilt about.

"Steal my son, bitch?" the raspy voice booms, a second pair of robot arms emerging from under the bed and flicking out towards Steph.

Steph starts to back away. Trips. The arms pick her up.

And tear her in two.

"That was no suicide," Nora says, trembling, collapsing into the chair in front of Jack's desk. "That was murder. You just murdered some one... We all murdered someone."

Jack puts his feet up on his desk. "Foster tells me otherwise. Reed signed the contract to kill himself. He pressed the button. That trigged the machine. Makes it suicide."

"Steph didn't sign anything."

"Yeah, that... Last minute thing. Let's just call it necessity-borne serendipity–really gave it that extra something." Jack smirks. "And she did sign something–the standard employee liability and permissions waiver. In case of tragic accident. Which, many people are going to testify this was. Who knew Reed knew was a closet robotics programmer, and crazy? Looks like we'll have to do a better job vetting in the future. Oh, well, lesson learned."

"This is insane. I feel... sick."

"Well, get it out of your system now. We're going to have to call the police here at some point. We edit the show, first, though." Jack taps the desk top. The flat switches on, already tuned to the closed-circuit of the stage. Blood everywhere, stage hands standing on the periphery gawking. "We time things right, the news should be hitting the net just about air time. Nobody's going to be watching the fuckin' Russians.–You know, I have to say, this is has been an extremely liberating experience. I'm oozing creative juices."

She stares blankly at him. He smiles back, paternal and sympathetic.

"Hey, none of that," he says. "Season finale's next week. We've got our work cut out for us–people are gonna expect something *really* big."

Three

WHEN THE SQUIRRELS AND PIGEONS HAD A WAR

KAFKA LIKES THE WARMTH best, but that's because she's fat and old, almost seven, and the wonders of the backyard had lost their appeal over the long, lazy years. She is satisfied to hang half on the sill above the kitchen sink, bask in the afternoon sun and enjoy the cool May breeze coming through the open window. She's spent the last hour toying with a one-winged fly desperately attempting to escape her by throwing itself comically against the screen.

But Elvis isn't one year old yet, and everything in the backyard still seems new to him. He sits on the sill and cleans himself, keeps sharp eyes out for any movement, anything of interest. Could be as simple as the breeze tearing a leaf off the gnarled pear tree or the sun striking one of the few unbroken windowpanes in the old, disused detached garage on the alley. Elvis is easily amused.

A squirrel more than amuses.

Elvis snaps to attention as the squirrel quickly spirals down the trunk of the pear tree, leaping the last few feet to the ground. Doesn't stop moving. It scuttles between two exposed roots, crouches low out of sight.

Seconds pass, and Elvis, thinking the excitement is over, is ready to dive back into cleaning the dirt and dust from a morning's worth of basement shenanigans out of his fine black fur. But out in the yard, the squirrel's ears crest the root. Slowly, its head rises until its eyes can see over the root, and it swings its head back and forth, scanning the backyard for something. Sniffs the air suspiciously. Spots the two pigeons watching it from their high perch on the garage's rain gutter. Ducks back behind the root.

Elvis is intrigued. The squirrel's being especially furtive, even for a squirrel.

Cleaning can wait.

Elvis leans forward, whiskers pressing against the screen, as the squirrel jumps high and wild, clearing the root entirely. Lands and makes a series of short hops, zigzagging across the back yard in an almost random pattern, yet ever so slightly in the general direction of the garage. The hopping goes on like this for a minute, until it eventually brings the squirrel very close to the garage. It looks around, sees how close it is, then quickly takes another hop. Away. Once on the ground again it spins in circles, chases its tail.

Elvis has never seen a squirrel behaving quite so oddly. Maybe Kafka has. "What's it doing?" he asks her, eyes fixed on the squirrel.

Kafka doesn't look up. Her attention is firmly on the helpless fly, trying a new tactic of escape by walking around the corner of the sill feeling for an exit it can't see. Kafka is giving the fly some headway, leaving it be so it develops a false sense of confidence. More interesting that way. "What's what doing?"

"That squirrel."

"It's a squirrel. Who knows? Not a one of them is all there. Don't have the sense to let themselves be domesticated."

In the yard, the squirrel stops running circles and rears up on its back feet, facing the garage. Small upper arms move in tiny circles, paws claw at the air. It makes hissing, clicking noises at the garage. No, not at the garage, Elvis realizes. At the pigeons on the gutter edging the roof. The pigeons aren't watching the squirrel any more. To Elvis, looks like they're making every effort not to look down and acknowledge what's going on below them. Elvis suspects this is more than the usual pigeon arrogance, but he can't think what.

Kafka hears the sounds the squirrel is making, finally decides there's something worth shifting her considerable weight around for. She lifts her head to look into the yard. "Well, that is unusual," she says after taking in the scene. The look on the old calico's face tells Elvis Kafka's never seen anything like this before, either.

What happens next is just as curious and unprecedented in either of their experiences.

A third pigeon swoops down from somewhere, nowhere–the sky. A fast, full power dive. Straight at the oblivious squirrel, desperately trying to get the attention of the pigeons on the gutter with a determination Elvis wasn't aware squirrels possessed. The swooping pigeon comes at the squirrel from behind and the squirrel never knows what's hit him. What's killed him.

Pigeon pulls up after striking, a leisurely arc back into the sky, the squirrel's head in its beak. The pigeons on the gutter are watching now, sure. Laughing it up.

Headless, the squirrel's body collapses to the ground. From high up in the pear tree come surprised moans and cries of shared pain. Squirrel moans, squirrel cries. The sound frighten Elvis to his bones. He arches his back, lets out a hiss of fear.

"Calm yourself, child," Kafka says, surprisingly detached.

"But... you saw... it was... horrible."

Kafka blinks. "Nothing compared to what's coming."

"What's coming?" Elvis asks, body relaxing although his heart continues to race.

"By the look of it, I'd say the pigeons have just declared war on the squirrels." She stamps a paw down hard on the one-winged fly, crushes it. Looks out into the backyard warily. "Not that it hasn't been a long time coming—the squirrels have been awful haughty lately. But one thing's for certain, scenery's about to get more interesting, tell you that much."

Elvis is awake and at the kitchen window before dawn. Been his routine the last week, watching the war unfold. He's left it to Kafka to wake the humans for breakfast since the war ramped up. That was always something Elvis enjoyed, looked forward to, the humans each morning getting into the spirit by feigning annoyance with his playful jumping on their heads and lying full on their faces so they couldn't breathe. But the war has held a deeper fascination for him, and for now, he has decided not to squander time on routine. He doesn't want to miss any more of the war than he must between naps and food.

This morning, he almost wishes he had gone to wake the humans. Then he might have been spared the sight, and the nightmares he's sure it will inspire every time he sleeps for a long time to come.

The backyard is a field of smoking craters and dead bodies, some places two or three deep, the results of a long and drawn out night of battle. Squirrels lie twisted and torn, limbs ripped off by beak or claw or the explosive-tipped bullets the pigeons prefer. Pigeons lie where they plummeted from the sky, their bodies riddled with the buckshot the squirrel anti-air gunners kept the sky thick with. There are more squirrel bodies than pigeon bodies. That's been the trend.

But there is some life in the backyard yet. Not squirrels or pigeons, but crows, dozens of them. Picking at the bodies of the dead, squirrel and pigeon alike, feasting with no shame. There's so many crows, and their war-time scavenging by now so down-pat, the yard will be picked well clean before the humans get out of bed. It will be as if nothing has happened, except in Elvis' nightmares.

Elvis can imagine the taste of pigeon, of squirrel, and the fact that the thought doesn't immediately disgust him tells him he's probably been paying too much attention to the war. Unhealthy, but he can't help himself. He hasn't eaten yet today.

"How's the war going this morning, child?" Kafka asks as she pulls herself onto the sill, her bulk forcing Elvis to make room for her. Then she sees for herself, and for a moment, her natural calm and good-humor leave her voice. "They're madmen. All of them."

Elvis' tone is hushed and respectful. "There must have been some kind of major assault. Looks like the squirrels made a push." It helps to not talk about the deaths, just the big picture, what Kafka calls it.

"I don't think so," Kafka says, laying down on the sill. Elvis can tell she's thankful for the change of topic. "Look how the squirrel casualties are arranged—like they were trying to surround the garage, dig in. Wouldn't have dug in if they planned to press ahead."

Discussing the war's ebb and flow has become a pastime with them. They talk of strategies, successful and failed, of what moves each side might take next. Never of when it might end. That would remind them that someday they won't be able to indulge in their new hobby.

"But why dig in?" Elvis asks. "The creeping-vine fence and black-berry bushes behind the tree would give them a highly defensible position."

"Don't know. Can't understand the squirrels, sometimes. Hard to think down to their level. Maybe they're trying to confuse the pigeons with illogical maneuvers."

Kafka's voice trails off as the sharp pop-snap of a dozen gunshots break the serene morning quiet of the yard. The crows instantly take flight. There's nothing in the backyard to fight over, worth risking their own lives for. There'll be plenty of food to come back to tomorrow.

The gunshots had come from the sky. Elvis and Kafka look up, watch as a trio of pigeons, a field commander flanked by two heavily-armed marines, swoop down to land dead-center in the yard. The marines sweep heads and guns in semi-circles, covering the officer as he heads for the body of a squirrel. A particular squirrel, bypassing closer and less torn apart ones.

The officer bends over the corpse, and Elvis thinks for a moment he's going to have himself a snack, but the officer merely plucks a satchel from the pigeon's waist with his beak. Pulls it hard, rough, no respect for the dead, snaps the tiny strap. Then satchel tight in his beak, the officer unfurls his wings and leaps into the air. The marines take a final look around and follow. The three fly fast at the garage, last second dive through an open, broken window pane. After they've gone through, other pigeons cover the pane from inside with a sheet of reinforced cardboard, holes poked in it for rifle barrels.

"What was that all about?" Elvis asks.

Kafka shrugs. "Whatever, won't be good for the squirrels."

The war continues unabated for days. Every night, Elvis and Kafka sit on the sill, watch the battles, one side making headway, the other side taking it back. When it began, it was an even fight, both sides having the same chance. The squirrels had numbers to compensate for the pigeon's command of the air. But nothing stays even forever, Elvis knows that much. One side was bound to get the edge, start their inevitable way to victory.

Elvis thinks the pigeons will come out on top, and some night soon, now. Kafka won't say who her pick is, likes to hedge her bets, but Elvis knows Kafka agrees with him. No contest, anymore.

Tonight's action is only making him more confident he's picked the eventual winner. It's been a brutal, bloody evening. Started with the pigeons in legion filling the sky to take the bushes along the alley fence. They met with no real resistance, slaughtered the few dozen squirrels defending it in the first minutes. From there it went further downhill for the squirrels. Whenever any poke their head out from a trench or from behind the safety of a tree-branch pill-box, a pigeon sniper in the garage is waiting to pick them off. There's been a lot of picking off, a lot of proud pigeon snipers.

"Their hearts don't seem in it," Kafka observes.

"Bet losing the back fence has demoralized them—after what they've been suffering, wouldn't need much of an excuse."

"Or there's something else going on."

"Like?"

Kafka shakes her head, begins cleaning herself.

The answer to Elvis' question comes about ten minutes later, but not from Kafka.

A barrage of missiles streak from the top of the squirrel stronghold pear tree to the garage. Explode before impact, spread tiny sharpened stones and rusted strips of scrap metal salvaged from around the neighborhood in pretty, puffy clouds. Plenty of light and sound but not much damage being done–Elvis doesn't think that's the intent, anyway. They're flak missiles, designed to keep the pigeons from the air by filling it with shrapnel.

Yes, the squirrels are definitely up to something.

Under cover of the suppression fire, squirrel troopers file down from the pear tree and out from the blackberry bushes. They form into a line, each trooper extending the line at the end by squatting down, leveling their rifle at the garage. As the line grows, Elvis sees it's going to stretch nearly to the house. Maybe all the way to the house, end up next to it, right under the kitchen window.

"What're they doing?" Elvis asks. "They can't be doing what it looks like, can they?"

"They are," Kafka says, sighing. "This will complicate things."

The line is soon complete, and it does run all the way to under the window. The troopers keep their guns on the garage, eyes trained for snipers because the pigeons aren't letting this maneuver go completely unchallenged. They may not be able to take to the air, but the pigeons can fire from the safety of the garage. The pigeons pop out from random sniper holes for mere seconds, pick their targets, fire, pop back in. The squirrels return fire, but by the time they do, there's nothing there for them to hit, and more squirrels have holes in their heads. Elvis figures half the squirrels in the line will be dead before five minutes are out.

Those kind of casualties, and for what? It can't simply be an exercise in futility or extremely bad tactics. Elvis looks at Kafka. The calico smiles back. She's figured it out, or thinks she has. "Wait." She points with a tilt of her head. "Look–the tree."

A small group of squirrels, perhaps a dozen, hunched low on all fours, move quickly out from the base of the pear tree. They aren't soldiers. Wearing badly-fitting helmets but not carrying weapons. Most are too small, would have trouble holding a rifle, or even a pistol. They're children, all but one of them. An adult female is in front, leads them across the yard behind the line of troopers providing them cover, and being rapidly picked off for their efforts.

Elvis stares unbelieving as the group hurriedly makes their way to the house, pigeon bullets many times nearly hitting one of them, forcing them to weave and causing one of the smallest squirrels–couldn't be more than a few weeks old–to panic, detaching from the pack and running out into the open. The adult moves like lightning to circle round, corral the baby back, while keeping the others moving forward.

After what seems like hours, but couldn't be more than a minute, the group reaches the house. Elvis can't see them, but he hears squirrel claws scrambling up the wall. Towards the window, Elvis realizes with shock.

The firefight abruptly stops.

Pigeons won't fire at the house. They know better than to involve the humans in the war, bad for everyone, especially the pigeons.

The squirrels should know better as well. Coming to the house–it's a breach of the oldest protocols. Wild and domesticated species don't mix, don't talk. Not done, not proper. There are rules that go back thousands of years. The squirrels must truly be desperate.

The squirrels crowd onto the short sill on the other side of the screen. The female stands up on her rear legs, to be eye-to-eye with

Elvis and Kafka, the children huddled around her. Under their helmets they are scared and shaking and Elvis knows they don't really understand what's going on, or why. They're just kids.

Just like him.

"Stay back, child," Kafka whispers, and Elvis does as she says. He gets down from the windowsill onto the counter, ducks into the darkness behind the toaster. But he makes sure he can see the window. He'll stay back, but he refuses to miss this.

"What do you want here?" Kafka asks the female adult disdainfully.

The female squirrel looks straight into Kafka's eyes. This is tough for her, and it shows. "It shames me, but I—we—must ask for your help."

Kafka shows no emotion, not that Elvis expected her to. "There's nothing we can do for you."

"You can protect our children. The pigeons will never come in the house." The squirrel lowers her eyes. "They'll be safe within its walls."

"You misunderstand. There's nothing we will do for you."

The female squirrel's face briefly becomes angry, then terribly sad. "You've seen the risks we've taken. The children, this isn't their war."

"It's not mine, either," Kafka says. She waves a dismissive paw at them. "Go, and don't ever come back."

The adult glances behind her. She knows what it means to leave the windowsill, make their way back to the tree. They'll be at the mercy of pigeon fire, the squirrel troopers that provided them cover dead or dying now, and no more to take their place. She turns back to stare at Kafka with desperation in her coal-black eyes. "Please..."

Kafka turns his back on them and steps down off the sill. "Don't make me involve the humans."

Knowing it's over, the female draws up her resolve, herds the children silently down over the edge of the sill.

Elvis wonders if he'll ever see them again. If they'll even live to get back to the tree.

—————

Elvis finds Kafka curled up on a comfy seat cushion on one of the kitchen table chairs. Sleeping like a baby. Like Elvis should be sleeping, but can't, because every time he closes his eyes he sees the faces of those poor squirrel kids, frightened and on the verge of tears, and the adult with her face drained of any hope or optimism as Kafka turned them away. How's he supposed to sleep with that running in his head?

The chair is pulled out some, so that Elvis can lie on the table above it, hang over the edge. Bat a paw not-so-lightly at Kafka's gray and pink nose.

Kafka doesn't open her eyes. "What?"

"I couldn't sleep."

"Well, I wasn't having any problems."

"What do you think'll happen to those squirrel kids?"

Kafka looks up at Elvis and shakes her head impatiently. "They'll grow up and become great military leaders, hardened by life's cruel inequities, and lead their people to eventual victory."

"I'm serious."

Kafka sneers. "They'll likely die. Tonight. Tomorrow. Won't last the week, my guess. The pigeons are winning, won't be long until it's all over. Is that what you wanted to hear?"

"Then why didn't you let them in? They'd be safe in here."

"Last thing we need running around here are orphans—and orphan rodents at that. Chewing wires, eating our food. Crying day and night for their parents who are never, ever coming back for them. You think the humans would allow that? You think we should?"

Elvis knows he should nod, but he can't help himself. "We could have hid them from the humans. And I would have taken care of them, you wouldn't have had to do anything, shared any of your precious food."

"This isn't about food."

"Then what is it about?"

Kafka sighs. "Listen, the squirrels have brought this on themselves. Helping them would only hurt them, give them false hope."

"Not to mention inconvenience you."

"Which is infinitely more important." Kafka stretches, languidly slides off the chair. Elvis looks down on her with no small amount of contempt and disgust. "Oh, don't give me that look," Kafka says. "You're young, you don't know better. Don't ever take what happens out there personally. It has nothing to do with us. Now, I'm going down to the basement–there's a spider's nest I've a mind to play with. You're welcome to come, watch an expert at work. You'll learn something."

"I think I'll stay up here a while," Elvis says, barely restraining the temptation to add *because I can't stand to be in the same room with you*. Instead, he says, "The moon's out, it's interesting."

Kafka is suspicious. "I think you'd better come along. Wouldn't want the screen accidentally opening."

"It won't. I won't. I swear," Elvis says, but even he isn't entirely convinced.

Outside, the night lights up. Whistling rockets, fireball flashes. The sounds shake the cups in the cupboard, rattle the plates.

"See, they're already at it again," Kafka says, shaking her head sadly. "They're doomed, all of them. Best to leave it alone."

With that, Kafka bounds down the stairs into the basement. Elvis lays on the table, listens to the explosions outside. After a moment, slips down to the floor to follow Kafka.

─────────────────────

The next night's assault begins with a sky filled with flak missiles, hundreds, thousands of screaming rockets arcing up from the pear tree over the garage.

A constant barrage, goes on forever, seems like to Elvis, giving the squirrels time to mass at the base of the pear tree, the only ground they haven't yet lost to the pigeons. Elvis didn't think the squirrels had the resources left to sustain such a barrage.

Elvis sees that some of the squirrel troopers in the mass are women. There are children, too. Armed children. He recognizes a few of them from the other night. They stood at the window and made him feel guilty.

Elvis immediately understands. This is either the squirrel's final bid for victory, or their final stand. Whichever it is, the war ends tonight.

Elvis calls for Kafka. The calico would never forgive him if he let her miss it.

Kafka steps up onto the sill, nods at Elvis. She had rushed up from the basement and has a ruined cobweb hanging from her whiskers. Doesn't say anything. She must sense the importance of the events in the backyard, doesn't want to ruin the moment with conversation.

Once massed, on some unheard signal, the squirrels begin their advance under the umbrella of flak keeping the sky clear. They move towards the garage. Intend to storm it, most likely. Marching methodically, with silent determination. The squirrels at the perimeter of the army keep a steady rate of rifle fire going at the sniper holes in the garage so that no pigeon dare try to get off a shot.

Elvis thinks if they keep it up, along with the flak missiles, the squirrels just might have a chance.

Pigeons must think this, too, as they open a section of roof despite the flak fire–they aren't about to let such a close victory be stolen from them this late in the war. A half-dozen pigeons, big ones, stern ones, flutter up from the hole, hover above the roof fearlessly, as if they aren't about to be ripped to shreds by the suppression fire. Doesn't seem to bother them in the least. The hole in the roof closes under them and they strike a missing-man formation, head out for the squirrel army.

These pigeons don't look right to Elvis. They've got some kind of armor over parts of their bodies–no, Elvis realizes, not over their bodies but as part of their bodies. These pigeons have made themselves part machine, all the better equipped to win the war.

The flak from the suppression missiles just bounces off these new-model pigeons–they fly through it with no more concern than if it were harmless dust. Steady and business-like, they pass over the squirrel army and sweep emerald green shafts of light emanating from their machine-eyes through the tightly-packed squirrels below. Wherever the beams touch, things burn, get cut in half. Mostly squirrels.

The squirrels do their best to return fire, to do something, anything to slow or stop the half-machine pigeons, but the squirrel rifles are no match for the metal skin and the beams of instant death. It's all the squirrels can do to keep their army together, keep themselves from panicking and running away.

Elvis wonders why they don't scatter, try to find cover. Obviously they're going to all die if they stay out in the open. Their march for the garage is over, no way they can stand against the machine pigeons.

They're waiting for something. But for what?

A whining whistle, high-pitched and loud, hurts Elvis' sensitive ears. He turns to look and sees arcs of flame rising from behind the vine-fence. Kafka lets out a gasp of surprise as she sees them, too, and sees at the same time that they aren't suppression rockets. They're squirrels.

Strapped into bulky harnesses, rifles in their forepaws, each carrying an apple-sized bundle stitched together from potato-chip bags and candy wrappers hanging in the tight grasp of their rear paws. Those would have to be bombs, Elvis decides.

The flying squirrels don't look like they can steer well, if at all. The air isn't natural to them, and all they can do is flail with their bushy tails and hope to keep on their flight paths–anything more than basic aerial maneuvers are out of the question. The half-machine pigeons are bypassed–they aren't the targets the squirrels had in mind. They've aimed themselves at the garage when they launched, and that is where they'll end up, with any luck.

Somewhere along the line the squirrels have stopped their suppression fire. To keep from killing the rocket squirrels. The pigeons have noticed this, and are quickly opening window-panes and roof holes so they can launch a counter-attack of pigeon troopers.

Elvis smiles as he figures it out. That's exactly what the squirrels must have been planning on.

The first of the rocket-squirrels hits the roof head-on, rocket-pack going full-thrust and the force of the impact knocking the wind out of the poor thing. Dazed, the squirrel barely manages to get a claw hold before sliding off the roof. It crawls back up to latch onto the edge of a roof hole. Executes this little back-arch flip, tosses the bundle-bomb around and into the hole. Lets go of the edge, falls off the roof with a triumphant yell. Flies straight at the ground, the rocket pack helping him along. No off switches, Elvis figures. Bad for the squirrel, the impact'll kill him.

The rest of the squirrels land better, scramble towards the closet open holes, throw their bundle-bombs down through. Jump back into the air. Pigeon snipers take out most of them as they retreat, dead or dying squirrels atop flaming jets of fire on random trajectories, but it doesn't matter. Their mission is accomplished.

Seconds go by, too many, until Elvis thinks nothing's going to happen. The whole thing valiant but futile in the end, more bad luck for the squirrels, seems to be their lot. He turns to Kafka, to ask her what she thinks, but a series of explosions deep inside the garage captures his full attention before he can speak. By the time he looks back at the garage the whole front wall is caving outward, fire and smoke rushing from the seams.

The squirrel army, what's left of it, lets out a cheer. Then a moan, as hundreds of pigeons come pouring out of the collapsing garage with the smoke, descend on the squirrels, beaks and claws powered by a need for revenge no bullet can match.

While their flesh-and-blood brothers take care of the squirrel army, the half-machine pigeons form up in a circle around the pear tree, concentrate their eye-beam fire on its trunk near the base. Their home is in ruins, time to return the favor. The old wood cuts easily.

A high-pitched whistling up in the sky, up real high. One of the rocket squirrels coming back down. Fur wet with blood from sniper bullets but it's still alive enough to try to control its descent. Looks intent on slamming into one of the machine-pigeons, do what little it can to stop the tree from being cut down while it has the chance.

Before it can get close, the half-machine pigeons hear the whistling. One turns its eye-beams away from the tree, up at the squirrel hurtling at it. The beam easily pierces the squirrel's side, goes right through, nicking the rocket pack. Sends the squirrel on a new course.

Straight at the kitchen window.

The squirrel, it's rocket fuel tank ruptured and misfiring wildly, screams and throws its paws up in front of its face as it rushes at the window. Elvis stares, stunned and unable to move, but Kafka's self-preservation instincts are more honed. She slams a paw hard on Elvis's head, pushes him down, and ducks herself.

The screen buckles inward as the squirrel hits it. He takes it along with him as he tumbles, crashing hard onto the kitchen table. The highly volatile fuel spills from the rocket tank, catches a spark.

The explosion knocks Kafka from the sill, spins her back into the yard.

Elvis manages to dig his claws into the sill and hunch tight. The kitchen on fire and filling with smoke, he apprehensively looks down into the yard and sees Kafka. Alive, shaking dust and smoke from her fur, as if everything's normal, nothing unusual going on.

"Come on, then, child," Kafka calls up at him. "It's not safe in there anymore."

Elvis isn't in the mood to think for himself. He jumps down into the yard without looking back.

There's no war going on out in the street. As if there's an invisible line somewhere between the front of the house and the back, and a whole other world lies on this side, one the war can't reach, can't effect. Like the one Elvis thought separated the backyard from the kitchen, but he doesn't want to think about how easily that wall crumbled.

Elvis stands cautiously on the sidewalk, catches his breath, and looks down the street. Tightly-packed houses, comfortable in their closeness. Nice houses, nice like his house was before the morning's chaos. Not burning, sending black smoke into the sky. Porches overflowing with flowers and proudly displaying colorful flags and decorative banners that flap gently in the wind. Peaceful. He wonders how long that will last. "What do we do now?" he asks no one in particular.

Kafka walks up to Elvis' side, sits. Casually begins her cleaning routine. "You do the honors. Pick one."

"Pick?"

"We need a new home, don't we? If we get one before breakfast, that would be especially nice."

"Just like that?"

"Get the right human answering the door, yes, just like that."

She makes it sound like this kind of thing is normal, just another thing cats do. Reassuring, what Elvis needs right now. Maybe everything will work itself out after all. "Any preferences?"

"One without a dog–that's a given. Don't need the headaches. And if it's all the same to you, I could live without a backyard."

Elvis nods. He'd already been thinking that, too.

Four

EDGY AND THE VOID

Edgy and Void in wait state.

Sitting on the steps of the Cathedral of Knowledge, Edgy propped up between Void's legs. Void's left hand—the one with the elaborate Celtic tattoo and missing middle finger—stroking Edgy's stringy, bleached white hair.

Twenty after two in the morning, watching homeless and tourists dancing around a wiccan fire in front of the old Shriner temple.

Their debit card is bulging. Night only half over and they've managed to scam nearly three million nuevo-francs.

They love tourists. The Solstice brings them in from the suburbs in flocks for a two-week long celebration of post-modern pseudo-primitivism and glorious, patriotic consumerism. Pray and spend.

Edgy and Void made their money selling worthless dispensations to the hapless tourists at a dozen nuevo-francs each. A simple scam, Edgy'd wave his hands over the buyer and mumble something indistinct. The tourists would laugh, smile, happy to play along. Figured it was charity. They'd pass their card to Void, and she'd touch it against a home-built reader. The little holographic screen would say TWELVE TRANSFERRED, a lie that wouldn't be noticed until the tourist tried to buy something else and discovered an empty card.

Now Edgy and Void are on breather. They've already made enough to get them through the next week. Food and drugs. And it's only the first night of Solstice.

Void takes a plastic vial from a torn pocket in her precisely tattered vintage Member's Only jacket. She holds it under Edgy's nose between finger and thumb, crushes it. The invisible contents spark, fizz, react with the air. Edgy snorts at wisps of yellow smoke.

Nice, Edgy says. Not out loud. To himself. And not in so many words. Just the emotion. The rawness.

Void reels, rolls her shoulders, smiles languidly as the drug hits her. She isn't much for doing drugs directly. She prefers the filter of another nervous system, the value-added rush.

Reflex, she brushes the transmitter stud at the base of her lover's skull, and reaches up to touch her own. Shiny, smooth nub. 900 MHz short-range packet switching modem.

Edgy shudders. "I feel..."

"Bored," Void finishes.

"Yes." He says it with more emphasis than is needed. He chuckles and Void feels him thinking: Good drug.

"What to do?" she asks. "There's always the Kast."

"Don't feel like alcohol. Depressing."

"Everyone will be there."

"Like I said–depressing."

"Then what?" Void asks.

Images flood her consciousness. Some, the vivid ones, come over the link. Edgy's the imaginative one. The artist. Scenes of orgies, setting graffiti nanochines loose inside the Carnegie, hiring a transvest whore to mock-rape tourists. Her own ideas are of a less ethereal nature. Jumping off the Three Rivers. Stealing a rent-a-cop car and cruising for nuns.

Hundreds of quick-cut flashes of possible evening entertainments pass between and through their minds.

The exchange takes all of a few seconds until one image remains in both their minds, shining, pulsing. Warm.

"That's the one."

Edgy chuckles. "Yep."

"Ain't no way you can be telling me you think that." That from the Korean behind the rental counter, playing with the old-fashioned cash register. Feeding it a new roll of receipt paper. "Travolta was toilette-bowl before *Pulp*."

"Bullshit he was," says the bald Puerto Rican leaning against the counter. He's leafing through a web page on a vid-plate. "You seem to be conveniently forgetting *Look Who's Talking Now*."

"You is so fuckin' insane. Damn dog movie." The Korean rings up a customer. "My man Sam carried Travolta. I mean on his shoulders, hopping on one foot."

Void listens to the exchange from across the video store, hovering between Indian musicals and Spanish adult cartoons. She picks up a random 3D-IHD case and absently reads the back while she waits for the conversation at the counter to resume. Something called "Willie Takes a Naughty Holiday", and a host of AI critics loved it.

Besides the Korean clerk and the bald Puerto Rican, three other Tarantinos mill around the counter. Two Cauks, both tall, one with short hair shaved in a one-inch square checkerboard, the other with a tight-curl blonde afro. The third's a chick–unusual for a Tarantino–and black, so gorgeous she makes Void a little envious. All wear jeans and Hawaiian shirts. Half their conversation is taking place over their head links.

The one with the afro. He's the Quentin, Void decides. Something in the way he holds himself. The distant look in his bloodshot eyes. He never speaks but the others glance at him, nod, or shake their head every so often.

Their link makes her become conscious of hers.

Across the street from the video store, sitting atop a mail box someone's filled with concrete, Edgy waits. Eyes, ears, nose, all his meat input, fed over the shared head link with Void. On her thighs, a phantom, Void feels the weight of the foot-long .22 caliber assassin bangstick with a twin ultraviolet laser sight waiting patiently in Edgy's lap. The sunglasses resting on his–their–forehead will let him–them–see the UV pinpoints, when the time comes.

Who? Edgy asks himself, and Void by link osmosis. Void looks up from the racks of videos. Her gaze settles first on Afro. The Quentin. But no, he's their hub, their server. Do him and their local network crumbles. No organization. Wouldn't be able to hunt worth shit. That's always a problem with the old protocols. Peer to peer's the way to go. Like her and Edgy.

So, next. Checkerboard and the chick are out. They both look fit. Work out, or do enough of the right drugs to achieve the same effect. Shame to waste that potential.

The Korean? No, the Korean mob is near the top of the food chain in Pittsburgh this summer. No sense taking chances starting a blood vendetta, too much heat in that. Not the kind of fun they're looking for.

That leaves the Puerto Rican. Yeah, he's the one. Pudgy. Wouldn't be much of a challenge in a hunt. Besides, he deserves it if he thinks the dog movie's a classic, Void figures.

Joy, excitement, anticipation, nervousness rolls through her. Partly hers, partly Edgy's. The mix is delicious.

Time to piss the fuckers off, get this thing going.

"Quentin Tarantino was a hack who wasn't fit to direct tampon commercials," Void announces, stepping out from behind the rack. "I laughed and laughed when I heard he'd got himself gunned down at the Oscars."

She pirouettes and at the completion of the spin flashes them the back of her left hand, fingers spread, her missing middle finger a canyon. Somehow that always seems so much more obscene than just a single extended finger. While they're staring, slack-jawed and eyes wide in shock and disbelief, Void turns, shoves her hands in her pockets, and hop-skips out of the store.

She sees herself through Edgy's eyes. Traipsing gingerly across the street, dodging a taxi, the Tarantinos coming after her, crowding through the doorway of the video store. She feels Edgy's lust for her long, lean body and the way it moves, and she smiles at that.

She brushes his knee as she runs past.

Again, seeing what he sees: The Tarantinos coming up behind her, charging after her. Checkerboard bounding onto and over the trunk of a powder blue hydro-Neon. Afro and the chick caught up short behind the same car. The Puerto Rican bringing up the rear, still not off the sidewalk. The Korean, loyal clerk to the end, is still inside, locking up the register.

Void's vision darkens as Edgy lowers the sunglasses over his eyes and raises the bangstick until twin ultraviolet dots sweep over the bridge of the Puerto Rican's nose.

Void stops running, spins to stand behind her lover. Now seeing the scene twice, through her own eyes and Edgy's eyes. Bad stereo-optic effect. Like a student film, or good drugs. She feels Edgy go to squeeze.

Still, she jumps when the bangstick goes off.Checkerboard has almost reached them but the noise and smoke stops him dead. He looks over his shoulder in time to see the Puerto Rican fall forward, plunge into the street, parts of his head arcing up like animé motion blur.

Stops traffic cold.

"Too cool," Edgy says, low whisper. Very pleased with himself. Void puts her hands on his shoulders, licks the back of his neck.

The death gets the attention of everyone on the street. The locals, who are interested just long enough to determine there's no immediate threat to their own safety, they soon go back on their way. The tourists, who gawk and ask inane questions to each other, amused by the show. The Tarantinos, standing still, standing like statues, in shock amidst the now frozen traffic.

Void giggles.

After a long moment or two the remaining Tarantinos and the more adventurous tourists congeal around the fallen Puerto Rican, forming the traditional stand-offish circle around the dead man.

Afro kneels over the body, checking vainly for a pulse. He doesn't find one. His face goes slack and he stands, head bowed. The other Tarantino's heads bow a moment later, and Void sees them trembling, trying to control some kind of inner scream of rage and disbelief.

While they're doing their funny little silent scream thing, three black and gray nanochine clouds converge above the body.

Void looks up, instantly sees the one cloud, the smaller, is an eye-and-ear collective. It stays floating above, recording the scene and sending a digital stream to news and tabloid outfits and to a host of public and private infonets. Void arches her back sexily for the cameras, and she feels the feedback loop from Edgy getting all tingly at her stretching.

The other, larger two clouds descend over the Puerto Rican. The crowd makes room, visibly afraid to get too near the morbid nanochines.

A swirling pixilated red cross within its constantly shifting form marks one of the larger clouds as a paramed unit. It swarms onto the body, sending tendrils of nanochines into what's left of the Puerto Rican's skull. It quickly determines the body is a corpse. With no life to save, it disengages, floats away back on patrol.

The second large cloud moves in. A scavenger collective, it engulfs the corpse. Strips away the Hawaiian shirt and jeans, tears the cloth into strands, then dust. Once the body is naked, the cloud eats away at the Puerto Rican's hair and epidermis, prepares the body for the meat wagon that will eventually come along to haul it to the recycling plants.

The nanochine stripping of their fellow gang member brings the full reality of the situation home to the Tarantinos and breaks them from their shock and mourning. It's time for revenge. Checkerboard leading the charge, they bolt across the street, head straight for Edgy and Void.

It's the moment Edgy and Void have been waiting for–the whole point of the exercise: The start of the hunt. Edgy slides off the mail box, drops the spent bangstick, and turns to follow Void, already skip-running away down the street, laughing.

Downtown. They'll lead the Tarantinos downtown, they agree over the link. The crowds will be large and fun to play with and around. With any luck they'll get there and find an orgy to disrupt while they're at it.

But the way downtown is blocked. By a traffic jam at the intersection. A dwarf in a Hawaiian shirt is standing on the roof of an SUV firing a long-barreled .357 Magnum randomly into the crowd. The chaos is impressive, and impassable.

Shit, Void thinks when she sees the dwarf and skids to a stop, another Tarantino, and Edgy swears out loud at the same time, stopping behind her. The Quentin, Afro, probably put out an all-points over their gang net and the dwarf's come running to help out. Blocking their way and letting out some frustration at the same time. Void expected the call for help to go out, but she wasn't expecting it to be answered so quickly. Could be a bad sign, like that it's all over already except for the hurting.

She steals a moment to tickle Edgy's pleasure centers. This is what makes it all worthwhile. The unexpected. The challenge.

They backtrack a few dozen feet to a nameless alley, duck down it. They don't have to look back to know the Tarantinos are following, even the dwarf, and probably a dozen other new ones besides.

The alley's short, a good quick run. They charge down it, pumping, making it rhythmic. Up ahead another crowd churns in a brightly lit street. They can lose themselves in that crowd. Good idea, they agree.

Approaching the street, Void wonders with a little disappointment why the Tarantinos aren't shooting at them. They're all packing, like the dwarf–it's part of their identity, their scene. They can't be worried about hitting innocent bystanders, can they? The crowd up ahead looks like tourists, and the city forces tourists to sign indemnity release papers to get in to Pittsburgh. So what's the deal?

As she and Edgy pump out of the alley and in to the partying crowd in the street, the reason why the Tarantinos aren't shooting becomes depressingly clear.

The street is filled with Hawaiian shirts and jeans.

It's a fucking convention.

There must be fifty of them, scattered amongst the tourists and pagans, and they're all partying, three or four Congo lines intertwining, an incestuous bacchanalia, the kind Solstice is known for. And the Tarantinos are apparently leading the festivities.

The partying Tarantinos don't react to Edgy and Void running into their midst, just keep on partying. Maybe they aren't aware of the chase. The Tarantinos' server protocol and its need for new members to be identified and handshaked into the ring can be thanked for that. Gives Edgy and Void a few seconds before the new Tarantinos will join in the pursuit. She knows they will join, only a matter of time, even though they're likely a different Tarantino faction. It's another part of their scene: A indiscriminate vengeful streak.

Edgy is already taking advantage of the precious seconds. She feels him push his way through a Congo line. A fat, naked pagan with bad breath pinches his ass. Coming up behind Edgy, following his lead, Void slaps the man playfully as she pushes past him herself.

Lying on the curb ahead of them, like a gift from the goddess, an electric bike. Edgy reaches it, tries to pull it upright. It moves maybe a foot, then stops hard. A loop of polycarbon chain runs from the frame to a drainage grate. Edgy curses.

Around them, the partying Tarantinos are becoming aware. Happy, blissful faces change to masks of anger and rage. Void can almost feel the pressure of all those eyes bearing down on them.

The Congo lines start coming apart.

New plan. Edgy is still cursing the bike, kicking it. Up to Void to figure something out. Meters up the street a pair of pre-pubescent suburbanites in store-bought homeless gear stand gawking, smokeless, non-carcinogenic cigarettes held awkwardly between overly lipsticked lips, skateboards tilted up on one edge, held against knees.

Void shrieks, throws herself at them. They naturally panic. So predictable. Drop their boards behind as they run away.

Edgy doesn't need to be told to follow or see the plan over their link. They're up on the boards and tearing away as the Tarantinos, each and every one, draw guns.

Huddled in the shadows of an alley off Pier Street. Hearts beating. Blood pumping. Alive. It isn't simply being prey. They'd popped a few vials as the boarded away from the street party. Stimulants this time.

All those Tarantinos. They hadn't really counted on so many when they'd begun this. The casual hunt had suddenly become something altogether more serious. They actually stood a chance of being caught. Didn't take the fun out of it, only took it to another level.

They're enjoying the new level.

Plans. Before it would have been a merry thing. Lead a half-dozen fanatics on a chase through the ruins of Pittsburgh, losing them easily before dawn. That plan was useless now–too many hunters to lose easily. They need another one. Quickly. Every Tarantino in Pittsburgh must be out looking for them, methodically searching. They need someplace they can weather the storm, until the Tarantinos get bored and just go away.

"Home," Edgy says. "Have to chance it."

Images of a squat concrete building, harsh white lighting, cold hallways, children's laughter, flood her senses. It isn't their place in the abandoned bunker on Squirrel Hill. Edgy means his first home. Where he'd been raised. The Anderson Crèche.

Void nods. She sends him an image of a forked road and darts down the alley. Edgy waits thirty beats then runs off in the opposite direction.

They leave the boards. Wouldn't be much of a hunt if they neglected to provide clues.

Void gets to the crèche before Edgy.

That doesn't particularly worry her. She knows the streets of the city better than Edgy does, been living on them longer than him. She can navigate with her eyes closed. Edgy gets lost going the bathroom, sometimes. She thinks that's charming.

Worries her more that they're out of contact, the link silent. She hates being alone with her own thoughts. No one else in her mind, feeding her data, extending herself. Isn't quite natural. If they live out the night she's definitely going to have to convince Edgy they need to get upgrades. Hundred meter transmit-receive range just isn't cutting it anymore.

She makes her way around the low fence surrounding the eight-story building. Between the fence and the crèche, which always reminds her of a stack of porcelain marbles, a twenty foot strip of seemingly bare earth. Edgy had shown her once what lives in that earth. She never wants to see it again. She isn't afraid of much, but the ghost-white things that broke the surface when Edgy lobbed a bag of White Castles over the fence scare her to the bone. Like giant maggots with mouths full of teeth. Better than land mines, protection-wise.

If Edgy's been caught, she'll throw herself over the fence. Real Romeo and Juliet moment. The thought chills and excites her.

She keeps walking as she passes the entrance to the crèche, hands deep in her pockets, head darting back and forth nervously keeping an eye out. From the dim archway in the fence leading to the revolving front door she hears the whine of a security camera tracking her progress. Slow, taking her time, she circles the building. Around her the neighborhood is quiet. Residential. Brownstones sided with armor plating. Middle-class, all in for the night.

On her third circuit she has a vivid daydream memory of the last time she and Edgy made love. This morning, subjective, around nine p.m., a quick, intense session while the espresso brewed.

The memory isn't hers, the images not what she saw, not with her own eyes. Edgy is coming. He's in range, sending her a hello and all's clear.

She quickens her pace and meets him at the front archway. He's already slotting his ident card. The indicator above the revolving door goes from red to amber to green, and they both sigh, relieved it still works. Edgy had walked away from the crèche when he was twelve. His card still works after five years because he has friends inside who tweak the custodian system once a month to make it believe he's an active resident, but you never know. People can get fired.

They hesitate long enough to kiss, then rotate through the front door.

Inside dormitory ten-twelve-em, it's sixty-seven degrees, twilight. White noise generators in the ceiling acoustic tiles drown out the snores of the four dozen pre-teens sleeping in autonomous therapy bunk beds lined along the circular wall. None of the boys are awake. The bunks see to that.

Edgy and Void don't bother being quiet. Relief at being safely in the arms of a government-strength security system is making them giddy. They sit on the floor between two empty bunk beds and break open a few vials. One stimulant, two euphorics. Not like they need the euphorics, but what the heck, they've cheated death a little longer, might as well make it a party, enjoy each other for a while.

They're stripping each other when the alarms go off.

The dim lighting snaps on stark and harsh and bright. The white noise becomes a warble, a whine designed to cut straight into sleeping minds.

"Fire drill?" Void asks, zipping up her jeans.

Edgy shakes his head. "Trouble. That's the fucking primo alarm. Nothing short of orbital bombardment's s'posed to set it off."

"Security breach do it?"

"If someone blew the front door, yeah."

They both imagine the same scene. Tarantinos with bombs, maybe a surplus rocket launcher taking out the revolving door. So much for government-strength security–but then the government isn't what it used to be, is it?

Around them boys are waking up, sitting up, jumping off their bunks. One by one their thoughts come on-line. In to her mind, uninvited.

Confusion. Fright. Uncertainty. Adventure!

Kid's thoughts.

Void slams her firewall into place before Edgy does. He'd grown up with so many disparate minds in his own, he's used to all the voices and is able to use that familiarity to gleam data before shutting off all connections but the one he shares with her, and a high-band-width special-purpose connection to the building's security system.

Edgy grabs Void's hand, pulls her up and towards a door. He shoots a picture of the crèche's floor plan to her, one he pulled from the security system. A bunch of red dots near the front door shows the Tarantinos. A blue dot, two floors up, is where they are. A third dot, green, pulsing, on the top floor. A dashed line traces the route from the blue dot to the green dot. Through the door they're running through now, up six flights of stairs.

"Should stay with the bigger kids," Void suggests as they bound up stairs two and three at a time. "Maybe they'll fight with us."

"No," Edgy says. He's panting. Too many euphorics. "They'll slow the fuckers down—but I asked them, they won't protect us if it means getting hurt themselves. They kind of resent me. They think you're hot, though."

Void smiles coyly. "Then?"

"Got an idea." They're at the top of the stairwell. A closed door is stamped DORMITORY FOUR-SEVEN M-F. Void tries the handle—locked from inside. She senses Edgy opening a hole in his firewall. A second later the door opens. A five year old in standard-issue coverall pajamas smiles up at them, stands back to let them in.

The autonomous bunks are smaller here. Three tiers, lining the walls. Children. Boys, girls, mostly blonde, some brunettes, sit on the bunks, or jump on them like makeshift trampolines. Others wrestle on the floor together, play handheld vidgames, giggle in small groups. None of them seem particularly alarmed that strangers are in their presence, or that they've been awakened in the middle of the night. But then again Edgy is helping them stay calm by sending reassuring thoughts into their local network.

Edgy opens the security system map in her head again. The red dots are blinking in dormitory ten-twelve-em. Void takes a moment to catch her breath, and notices Edgy is holding the door to the stairwell open, anxiousness on his face and coming over the link.

In her head a single small red dot breaks off from the big group and makes its way to the stairwell. Bad. Won't be long before the rest get through.

"Have to get the hub," Edgy says. "Stay here. Organize."

"Organize?"

Army camp. Basic training. Patton standing in front of an American flag. John Lithgow rallying the red Lectroids. Set-piece fight scenes from old Jackie Chan and Van Damme flatvids. She gets the idea.

"But they're kids, Edgy..."

Gunshots echo up the stairwell.

"All the better." Edgy kisses her cheek and ducks through the doorway. The door shuts and locks automatically behind him.

Void is instantly surrounded by kids, physically at least. Her firewall is still in place. The kids look at her expectantly, patiently, waiting for her to join their network. To play.

"Hi. I'm Void," she offers. She starts to slowly dissolve her firewall, cautious, then decides the caution is unwarranted–they are only kids after all–and just lets it go completely, all in an instant.

Mistake.

Adults in her mind are never a problem. Nights at the Kast with the gang sharing its drunken and drugged thoughts, trading in-jokes at the speed of synapses, that's the way a headpack should work. Even when everyone is stoned out of their minds some level of structure exists, an overlay of social order and general politeness there that helps keep everything under control.

But these kids, they don't think with much structure. Don't want to, don't need to. And peer-to-peer is so free-form to begin with. Edgy grew up with it. She hadn't. She hadn't even gotten her implant until she was ten, already a two year veteran of the streets. The rush of the kid's thoughts is too much.

Void's knees buckle. She sits down on the floor and the kids come closer, crowd her in the way kids do, like she's a wounded puppy. Each and every one of them is sending her questions, impressions, invitations. All innocent, and all of it a jumble, making things worse. They don't mean any harm, don't know better. Don't know there's an army downstairs.

Do over.

The firewall comes back at her bidding, wraps itself around her consciousness like a hazy, baby-blue security blanket. The kids nearest her wear disappointed expressions at being abruptly shut out. One looks like he's going to start balling.

The small red dot in the stairwell is joined by other dots. Checking every floor, every door. They've made it to the sixth floor. Two more to go, damn them.

In another part of her mind she's Edgy, going for the emergency exit in the dorm one floor down. Finding it, blowing the hatch, sliding down the outside of the building inside an inflatable escape chute. She has no doubts about his intentions. He isn't saving himself.

On the security map a number of dots converge on the door to the dorm where Edgy has hit the chute. Emergency exit must have tripped an alarm, and the Tarantinos must have heard. Explains why Edgy just didn't take the chute out of this floor. Subterfuge. Fuck she loves that guy.

Ready now. She draws herself up to her feet.

The firewall comes down again, only by slow degrees this time. Letting one or two kids into her mind at a time, as she does telling them to stay quiet until everyone is in.

Outside, the tube delivers Edgy softly on the safe side of the fence. He bends low, runs around to the front of the building. The revolving door is gone along with most of the doorway. Standing in the hole, just inside the lobby amongst concrete and glass shards, Afro sways slightly, as if trying to conjure up a wind. The movements of a hub in full server mode. His back is to Edgy. Wouldn't matter, anyway.

The red dots are all back together again, and right outside the door to dormitory four-seven em-eff. All the kids are in Void's mind now. And she in theirs. She has them playing a game.

Called R.U.R.. They're the robots, she the evil robot slave master. She nudges them back away from the door, joints stiff, jerky movements, has them pick up toys, vidgames, anything harder than a stuffed animal, preferably with a sharp edge or two.

Gunshots on the other side of the door. The metal around the door handle crinkles.

The door bursts inward. Checkerboard comes through the doorway, a matte black 9 millimeter Glock with a laser sight in his hands. Void's optimism at surviving the night vanish. She only hopes they won't hurt the kids.

Down in the lobby, Edgy comes up behind Afro raising a piece of masonry above his head. Edgy brings it down. Not as much blood sprouts out of the back of Afro's skull as prime-time television has led Void to expect. Working quickly, Edgy pulls the unconscious Quentin out of the lobby, right alongside the security fence, and with a bit of effort—it's been a tiring night all around—he manhandles Afro up and over the fence.

Afro lands with a soft thud.

Void knows what's coming next. Doesn't make it any easier to stomach.

Afro wakes up as the first of the things come out of the loose ground and attaches itself to his side. Really would have been better for him if he'd stayed out. Dead white flesh squirming in the moonlight, gnawing at his stomach. Afro screams and screams.

Void shuts her own eyes but that doesn't help. Forced to watch as Edgy does. Afro flailing at the oversized maggots leaping onto him. Doesn't take long, or much of a struggle. The creatures are through the Hawaiian shirt and his skin and exposing ribs when Edgy finally decides he's had enough and looks away.

The children see it through Edgy's eyes, too, passed straight through her. Their playfulness is instantly gone, replaced by the kind of abject terror only a six-year old can feel.

Caught up in a feedback loop of childish disgust, horror, and fascination, it takes Void a beat to notice the Tarantinos who'd come through the door have stopped advancing. Checkerboard has even lowered his gun. His face is blank, the blank of a really good drug. All of the Tarantinos are like that.

Their Quentin is gone. And they felt him being eaten alive. Felt it like they were being eaten alive themselves.

The confusion won't last long. They'll elect another Quentin. That blank stare is them voting. Void gets ready. For whatever.

Easy enough to convince the children the Tarantinos are bad men after what they've just seen, she just sends them a picture of the Tarantinos feeding kids to those maggot things. Even easier to convince the kids to rush. Nothing a kid likes more after a good scare than getting the chance to do some serious damage.

Her thoughts encouraging them, the kids advance. Small hands wielding toys, slamming kneecaps, jumping on backs, biting in to soft adult parts.

The Tarantinos aren't sure what's happening, except that they're surrounded.

Washing through her, the kids thoughts are more disturbing to Void than the scene of Afro being eaten. Edgy had killed to survive. The kids are tearing in to the Tarantinos because it's fun. And she'd gotten them to do it—easily. Most disturbing of all, she's enjoying the power, the control. Here she'd thought there wasn't a maternal bone in her body.

But now is not the time to get sentimental.

Void moves to the emergency exit on the other side of the room. She presses a bright red, child-friendly activation button. A pop of air and a section of wall crack to reveal a tube of plastic. The tube rustles loudly as it inflates and unrolls.

Crawling feet first into the tube, she brings the firewall back up, to shut out the gleeful thoughts of the children as they play.

She slides.

Edgy meets her at the bottom.

In her mind, a three-story building in the bad side of town, bricks covered with graffiti, a neon Iron City Light sign flickering in a dust-crusted window.

"The Kast?" she asks, caressing the image he's sending with warm fondness.

"Yeah," Edgy says, smiling. Every time he does that Void's stomach does happy flips. "Now I'm in the mood."

He slides his arm around her waist, and she dips her hand into his back pocket.

Five

THE CREDITORS

Earth declared bankruptcy August Seventh, 2018.

I actually watched the sign-over ceremony live. Something that historic, I figured it'd be a shame to only catch the highlights on FNCNN.

Naturally, they'd wanted to hold the ceremony in the United Nations building in New York, but it had already been sold off and razed for a parking lot by then. They ended up having to hold it in an appropriate alternate site, the U.S. Senate chamber. Never mind the Capital building had by that time been converted into a bed-and-breakfast for off-world tourists. An extra bonus for the aliens staying there, they got to personally witness the historic event over eggs and bacon.

It went down at Sunday brunch. A small group of humans and Creditors gathered in front of a buffet spread laid out on the raised desks where the officers of the Senate once held court, and there the leaders of the four remaining sovereign governments of Earth signed over the planet, and everything on and in it, to the Creditors.

There wasn't any applause from the brunchers, and certainly none from the decidedly somber humans, only the delicate scraping of segmented Creditor secondary limbs against each other. Their way of expressing either happiness or anticipation of profit. They'd never explained what the distinction was. Probably wasn't any.

And that was it. The Earth, humanity, everything, it all belonged to an alien race, for the foreseeable future, and probably much longer, when interest rates are figured in.

The invasion was over, and we'd let it happen without a fight–shit, it couldn't have succeeded without our complicity, truth be told. When it came down to it, we were basically fighting ourselves, and we lost. The Creditors just sat back and gave us the chance to be the pathetic, weak-willed creatures we always feared we were.

Couldn't really blame the Creditors for that–they were simply taking advantage of a business opportunity. It's not like they held a gun to our heads.

No, not guns. Just consumer goods.

When it started, we didn't peg it as an invasion. Anything but. The intelligentsia and the pundits, the politicians and the theologians, they saw it as nothing less than the next step in the evolution of humankind, a watershed moment wherein we realized we were not alone in the universe. Nobody even seemed to mind the kick-in-the-ego of finding out we weren't nearly the most advanced species out there. We were just another species in a universe filled with them. Nothing special. The debates and commentaries ricocheted ceaselessly through the media.

Us normal people, we didn't need to debate. We knew exactly what the Creditor's arrival meant. It would be the greatest shopping experience ever. That's what the ads promised, and we believed them.

In classic pulp fashion, the day they arrived, their fleet settling into geo-synch orbit, the Creditors simultaneously took over every broadcast channel, every web-site, every signal routing through every telecom sat, to get their initial message out. Only they didn't pre-empt by force. Instead, they actually paid for the time. Paid well, too, with the promise of many future ad buys at the same or better rates.

That was the first of many hooks they were able to sink into us, a promise the ad men and women of the world simply could not resist. The Creditors had hooks to appeal to everyone, and they eventually sunk them all.

The Creditors had known we were ready for them when one of their listening posts picked up the tell-tale stringspace signature of an artificial worm-hole being brought into existence. It hadn't been a big one, an after-hours, semi-drunken experiment by graduate students at MIT, and it only stuck around in our universe for a dozen nano-seconds, but it triggered the Creditor sensors in orbit around Peg Beta all the same.

The Creditors had littered the Milky Way with such posts, set to tirelessly scan the relevant frequencies. The moment the one in our sector of the galaxy got a whiff of our technological progress, the entirety of the vast Creditor organization mobilized to bring us into their community. As they had been doing with other planets, other species, for thousands of years. They had it down to a science.

The first Creditor malls touched down in India, Arizona, South Africa, South Korea, and next to Euro-Disney. More malls came later, until you were never more than two-hundred miles away from one no matter where you went. They all carried the same things, the same products, at exactly the same prices. It didn't matter which one you went to, only that you went, and bought. With the ongoing advertising blitz, and the sheer faddishness of the malls, few could escape the pull. Everyone visited, and no matter how hard you protested that you were only going to window shop, you inevitably bought something, inevitably on credit.

That's because credit was the *only* way to buy things at the malls. The Creditors didn't take dollars or yen or even gold nuggets. They weren't interested. They wanted to lock you into their own credit plans. The reason why became obvious only later, near the end.

Getting a Creditor mall credit line was easy enough. Every time you set foot in a mall, robot attendants would corner you if sensors in the doorways didn't detect a credit ID on you. They'd sign you up, a simple procedure where you press your thumb against a pad with infinitesimal writing on it, then hand you an ID and a copy of the agreement for you to read at your leisure. The robots wouldn't bother summarizing the agreement for you—that would have delayed your shopping experience. The most they'd tell you was that you'd know you had enough credit to buy something if the price tag went yellow when you held your ID up to it. You know, I never saw a price tag that didn't go yellow.

But that didn't matter. You weren't thinking about credit lines when you hit the mall proper. Once you first wandered the looping halls of a mall, got one look at the storefronts full of products from a hundred different worlds, a dozen different races, you were hooked. Age-old genetic imperatives kicked in, demanding you possess the latest, the greatest, the new and exciting, the status symbols. Besides, who could resist a robot butler that looked like Cameron Diaz and ran for three weeks on a nine-volt battery, especially if you didn't have to make any payments for a year, no money down?

That was the weird thing, the thing that should have raised every flag, given every consumer protection advocate on the planet a hard-on for the sound-bites they could generate off it. That damn payment plan where you not only didn't have to make any payments the first year, you couldn't, even if you wanted to. The Creditors claimed they needed the year to give them time to work out a fair exchange rate between earth currencies and their own. Funny thing is, the credit line agreement they made you sign made no mention of cash repayment, only a vaguely worded reference to repayment by "any and all commodities to be named and found of satisfactory value by Creditor."

Not even the governments of earth, with their oversight committees and buildings full of bureaucrats who normally reveled in questioning such things, pressed very hard for clarification on what type of commodities the Creditors had in mind.

The governments had their own concerns, I guess.

Consumer goods brought the masses in, but the malls sold other things, too. Things governments were interested in. Autonomous tanks with legs instead of tracks, surveillance systems that could read strong thoughts at twenty paces, riot-control ultra-sound sleepy-time projectors, sentient factories. All available on credit, with credit lines set by no more complex algorithm than desire–if a government wanted a particular piece of technology or device badly enough, the Creditors were more than happy to make the sale, provided the government secured the debt sufficiently. Usually that meant putting up land, or future tax revenue, or, as with the individual consumer credit lines, commodities to be named later.

The governments of the world signed away a lot of things as they kept buying and buying, starting a sort of cold war of one-upmanship. If one country had a fighter jet that could in-flight convert to a submarine, or something of equally dubious value, they all had to have it, or a better model.

Not surprisingly, the Creditors encouraged this behavior. They set up web sites listing every government purchase in real time, available for all to peruse. The purchase notices carried product specs, and naturally, pricing for all those other countries interested in keeping up with the Joneses.

It was quite a racket.

Every few months, the Creditors would introduce new merchandise or devices to upgrade the stuff the governments had already bought, and the feeding frenzy would start again with renewed vigor. The Creditors were pros at that sort of thing. They seemed to have a seventh sense about when the world was ready for another round of product upgrades.

They also seemed to know exactly when to start collecting the debt of the world. Maybe somewhere in the Creditor computer system where sales and debts were recorded, some magic number—a certain percentage of the Earth's total present and future worth—was reached. Or maybe the Creditors felt it in their exoskeletons as instinct. The time was right: For all intents and purposes they owned the Earth and we who lived on it.

Whatever the trigger, a year and seven months after the first mall opened, the Creditors started calling in our debts, and at last they announced what they wanted in payment. They wanted paid in land and labor. All our land. All our labor.

Humanity itself was the commodity to be named later.

They had a whole other species to do their collecting. Called them the Collectors, wouldn't you know. Where the Creditors looked vaguely like a cross between an elephant and a cockroach, the Collectors were all puffy and small, like boneless sacks of moles inter-bred with squid. Not pretty, but efficient. They had these mental powers that let them reach inside your mind and make you want to comply, want to pay your debt. It wasn't full blown mind control, more like they were able to inspire a nagging desire to make good on your commitments. All it took was for a few of the Collectors to ride through a neighborhood broadcasting and the Creditor coffers would begin to fill.

Some countries tried to resist, using their newly high-tech armies to defend their borders and skies from the Collectors. Futile, of course. Especially as it turned out every piece of Creditor technology had built into it circuits that wouldn't let it be used against the Creditors or the Collectors. Even going back to the good-old standbys of earth-made weaponry didn't do much. Bullets aren't exactly effective against species that have conquered faster-than-light travel and interstellar commerce.

After the first round of pointless armed resistance, most countries opened negotiations. It was obvious we'd dug our own grave and there wasn't much to do except jump on in.

Would you believe, even as the governments of the world turned over their property, their land, their citizens, they kept buying? The same thing went for individuals. I knew people who on the same day they handed their children over to the Collectors to become butlers, maids and general laborers for other Creditor-served species, went to a mall to buy more stuff.

Within a year, it was all over, and the Creditors got their wish. The signing ceremony went down and they owned us. Another successful, mostly bloodless invasion to enter into their books. Another world to convert into their ideal of perfection, where everyone worked for them, and everything was dedicated to producing products for their malls, so they could find other planets with populations to sell to.

Nice and tidy.

A few thousand of us managed to get away from the Earth, before the signing. To Mars, where there were no malls, no Creditors, only the pre-fabricated remnants of a failed Russo-Euro colony attempt from a few years before the arrival of the Creditors. This time we had Creditor technology–some bought, admittedly, but most of it stolen or rented from our fellow humans–to make a go at it. Alongside the abandoned reinforced-concrete domes we put our plastisteel, two story A-frame bungalows and grew automated food factories. Tried to make lives for ourselves and waited for the invasion.

I have to give the Creditors credit, they took their time, and they didn't even try to use military force. Not their thing. They ignored us up until a month after the ceremony in D.C., when they dropped a mall not-so-discretely at the base of Olympus Mons. Day and night the mall beckoned, hologram advertisements playing out in the sky. They even broadcast audio ads straight into our heads via induction, so our own bones sang the praises of shopping.

Let me tell you, there's nothing like waking up in a cold sweat after a nightmare where you're running wild through a mall buying everything that comes within arm's length at the behest of a chorus of encouraging, motherly voices and finding those voices still with you, ringing in your ears.

We found ways to block that soon enough. Then they started the real blitz. Pamphlet bombings. Door-to-door robot credit sign-up offers at three in the morning. Discounts. Clearance sales.

It is a constant barrage of enticements, but we persevere.

It's been a year, and it's been getting harder, but not one of us has broken ranks. Oh, sure, there are grumbles. Outpost council meetings are usually nothing more than gripe sessions these days. Supplies are running out, and either because of shoddy workmanship or hidden planned obsolescence circuits, some of the more useful Creditor technology devices we depend on are acting up, breaking down.

We're dying. Mars isn't the type of planet you can eke an existence out of without high technology. Working high technology.

We all know we'll need to go to the mall someday, probably someday soon. It's a question of survival, now. But nobody wants to be the first. Nobody wants to be the one to break, to have the others hang that kind of label on him. Traitor to the cause. Weak-willed consumer.

Human.

I know I don't. And I'll try to resist as long as I can, but frankly, I just ran out of nine-volt batteries for my robot Diaz.

Six

SECOND UNIT

ONE OF THE MORE unexpected things I discovered about space flight that first time was that I can't sleep in zero-gee.

I must have been floating in that bag at least two hours, twisting, writhing, and trying to force myself to sleep. The irony of it all was that I truly was dead tired.

I'd been up and running frantic for nearly thirty hours, starting with the shuttle trip up from Pasadena, to seeing that the recording platform was docked, loaded and secured, to taking care of the millions of last minute details always left to the A.D. because the director doesn't want to bother and instead wants to chat up the skipper of the tug hired to take us out. Running my head off, and looking forward to sleep the whole time.

Only when it got to it, after I'd checked to make sure we'd brought everything and the tow lines were all nice and tight, and I'd wrestled myself into the bag on the wall–floor, ceiling, whatever–of my cubicle-sized cabin, I couldn't do anything but stir there uncomfortably, my stomach constantly reminding me that it was going to get even, sooner or later, for what I was putting it through.

And of course, my luck being what it is, when I did at long last find myself drifting off to sleep, what sounded like every alarm and siren ever built by man went off, filling my cabin with a horrible, dissonant whine, as if a pod of whales was being squished painfully into a goldfish bowl just behind and to the left of my head.

Great place to put a speaker. If I ever got the chance, I'd have to have a word with the genius who designed the ship. Several words, with a big wooden stick providing the vocabulary.

The siren wasn't getting any quieter. I fumbled at the bag's zipper, getting it half-way down, just far enough for me to free myself and get away from the noise. I backed into the hallway, pushing myself along with my hands. The sirens weren't any better out there.

I flipped around, oriented myself, and then started pulling myself fore to where the skipper had shown me the Conn on the quick tour he gave after we boarded. I hoped to find the skipper there, and something to use to beat him with until he turned off the damn noise.

The skipper was indeed in the Conn, but there were no sticks, rods, or loose pieces of furniture for me to grab. Damn zero-gee: Everything was tied down. Just as well, though, since the skipper was a real big guy—not only obese, but muscularly obese—and he seemed to be having enough trouble on his own.

It was then, seeing the way the skipper was frantically clawing and clubbing at the control panels at the front of the Conn, that the possibility of the alarm signifying something other than the Universe's way of keeping me awake occurred to me.

To me, not experienced in the ways of real space travel, but thoroughly familiar with movies about space travel, a siren as loud and annoying as the one warbling through the tug ship could only mean one thing: We were about to die. My mind played out the possibilities for me, replaying dozens of scenes from movies I'd seen in my soon-to-be cut-short life. Perhaps our hull had been breached in an asteroid collision, or the nuclear power plant had had an unexpected meltdown, or an as-of-yet undiscovered species of space-dwelling giant tiger shark with a taste for starship hull composite had happened upon us just at his lunchtime. The last wasn't very likely, admittedly, but my madly racing panic didn't much care for presenting me with real possibilities. No, it was going for the really dramatic, if impossible, stuff. As if it wanted to go out on a high note of creative expression.

I floated in the hatchway, trying to see the displays past the bulk of the skipper, to get an idea of what form my death was taking. The skipper was panting, mumbling to himself, banging at the controls. He didn't look happy. Or clothed. A small measure of revenge: The siren had interrupted his sleep as well.

I didn't want to disturb him, to break his concentration --in case that was all that stood between us and death–but it didn't look as if he was doing anything constructive. His ministrations appeared to be pretty random. Desperately random. "Excuse me... but can I ask what's going on?"

The skipper didn't acknowledge my presence, let alone answer my question. He had stopped to listen intently to a faint computer voice announce: "You now have forty seconds to transfer funds. Self-repossession will occur in thirty seconds."

"Oh, great," said a voice from behind me. A female voice. Then, yelling past me: "I thought you were going to take care of that yesterday, Skipper?"

"Slipped my mind, slipped my mind," the skipper yelled back, turning around briefly then immediately returning to his desperate banging. "Where's the fucking card?"

"Under the console. Taped to the fire extinguisher," she said.

For a big guy he could move pretty gracefully in zero-gee. Instead of simply reaching under the console, he cartwheeled, re-orienting himself so his feet were pointing at the ceiling. His hands worked frantically out of sight for a few seconds then he cartwheeled again, back to his original orientation. Now in his stubby-fingered hand he held some kind of cash card and he waived it over the console as if he were looking for the right slot to stick it in.

"You now have fifteen seconds to transfer funds," the computer stated flatly. "Uragon-Marshall Corporate Financing would advise making payment at your earliest convenience. Failure to make payment will not reflect well on your personal or corporate credit records. You now have seven seconds."

"Left," the woman yelled to the skipper. "Above the secondary telemetry. The big red box."

"Oh, yeah." The skipper found the box and slipped the card into a slot. With a rushed flourish he slapped his palm against a built-in reader plate. The box beeped.

"One moment please. Contacting Uragon-Marshall Corporate for confirmation." A ten-second long pause, then the moment I'd been waiting for occurred. The sirens stopped. "Payment confirmed. Thank you for your compliance. The next scheduled quarterly payment is due twelve-hundred hours Greenwich mean, March Third, Twenty-One Thirty-Five. Have a nice morning."

The skipper pulled the card out, shoved it in the waistband of his underwear, the only thing he was wearing. He closed his eyes and let out a long whoosh of air.

"What the hell was that all about?" I asked him. He didn't answer, just shook his head and pushed past me.

He spoke to the woman floating behind me as he passed her. "I'm going back to bed, Mate."

I watched him pull himself down the hallway, then turned to the woman. "You're the mate?"

"Only in the nautical sense," she said, smiling. Nice smile. Nice everything now that I had a chance to look at her without sirens going off around me, ruining what little concentration I was capable of in my zoned-out, sleep-deprived state. I diverted that line of thought for the moment and asked her the same question I had asked the skipper, only more politely.

"Oh, that was just the bank's way of reminding us who really is the captain of this tug."

"Excuse me?"

"The ship is programmed to re-possess itself if we miss a mortgage payment. It'll pilot itself all the way back to the orbital yard using a whole independent control and thrust system if we're delinquent by even a second.—It would have cooked itself up a wormhole and slipped through non-space if it'd needed to. Bank's real serious about their money."

"Understandable."

"But real inconvenient when the skipper forgets to make the payments."

I nodded. "Annoying, too."

"Got that right. Sorry if it woke you up."

"Wasn't getting much sleep, anyway."

She spun, started down the hall. "Well, come on then. Got just the thing in the galley."

"Sometimes, I wonder why I work for the man," the mate said, showing me how to hook my foot into a loop in the wall so I could "sit" at the high galley table. It looked uncomfortable when she did it, and it proved as much when I did, but it kept me from floating away. She pushed off the table and gently collided with the opposite wall, where she opened a cabinet and took out a baggie of medium-strength Sleepy Beddy Time brand enriched powdered milk. "Sure, as bosses go, the skipper's not too bad. Gave me a stake in the tug: five-percent ownership. Didn't have to do that. But he's a little on the absent-minded side, you know? No matter how many times I remind him, he always forgets to pay the bills until the last moment. Usually we haul cargo, not people, so he's never embarrassed himself like that in front of passengers before."

"Don't worry about it. Like I said, I wasn't getting any sleep, and my ears will stop ringing eventually, I suspect. Besides, working for Prodamey I've gotten used to alarms in the middle of the night."

She pushed the baggie of powder through the air-tight slit on a pouch of water. The baggie, made of a neutral cellulose compound, almost instantly began to dissolve, releasing the powder into the water. She kneaded the pouch to mix it. "Still, must be interesting work, doing films."

"You'd think so, wouldn't ya? It's just a job, though. Got its high points and its low points. Like space travel. A low point, I'm sorry to admit."

"You get used to it." She put the pouch of reconstituted milk in the microwave and hit a few buttons.

"I don't see how." I offered a glib smile to her reflection in the microwave door. "But I suppose I will. If I can get used to Prodamey, I can get used to anything. They say you get used to hot needles in the eye after the first dozen."

"She's tough to work with? So the stereotype I'm always hearing about big-time movie auteurs being pains-in-the-ass is true?"

"Yeah, only problem is, Prodamey's no auteur. Shit, she isn't even a first-rank director. Just a rookie second unit director with an ego seven-hundred times the size that usually calls for."

The microwave buzzed and she popped the door open. "'Second unit'?"

"Yeah, that's what we are, me and Prodamey. The Second Unit. She's the second unit director, I'm her A.D.–Assistant Director. That's one of those job titles that looks good during when the credits roll but really means I'm a glorified gopher. And underpaid, even by gopher standards."

"Sounds like the very same job description as Ship's Mate." She tossed me the pouch of milk. I caught it cautiously, expecting it to be hot, but it was room-temperature. Either she hadn't nuked it long enough, or the pouch itself was acting as a pot-holder. "What exactly does a second unit do?" she asked, flipping a straw at me.

"Crap the real director doesn't want to bother with. Establishing shots, minor scenes with doubles or extras, cut-ins, sometimes stunts if the script calls for them." I pierced the pouch with the straw and took a sip. Hot. Just the right temperature, and only a slight aftertaste from the mix of mild sleep-aid narcotics and tranquilizers in it. "Before we boarded we were in South Africa, filming trees."

"Just trees?"

"Special kind of trees. In rain. And wind. And in the hot noon sun. Eventually the main unit director–a real auteur she is–will pick out one or two shots to use in the film, depending on the mood she wants for the scene. Or maybe she won't pick any at all. Three weeks down the drain. Movie biz is like that. I get paid either way."

"Nice work if you can get it, though?"

"Yeah. I've got one great union, so got that going for me, anyway." I took another sip of the milk. I could just barely feel the narcotics kicking in, like a spreading tingle of numbness at the base of my skull. "When do we get to the Lagrange point?"

"In a few hours. This morning sometime. If you want, I'll ask the ship."

"No need, I don't need to have an exact time. Just curious. Hopefully I'll sleep right through it."

"No bother. Anyway, you look like someone who could use a laugh." She turned her head towards the nearest wall. "Ship?"

"Online," responded a disembodied voice that sounded vaguely like Danny Kaye.

"What's our ETA to the Lagrange point?"

"ETA, Mate?"

"Estimated Time of Arrival."

"Oh, that. Give me a second." A long pause. "Well, funny thing, I don't know. Have no idea. Where is this Lagrange fellow, anyway? He aboard? I'm not showing him on the registry."

"Thank you, Ship, that'll be all for now."

"Offline," it said.

"That was supposed to make me laugh?" I asked.

She shrugged. "Well, makes me laugh—either that or I'd cry. Computer used to be pretty damn smart—a decent conversationalist, too, on those lonely long-hauls—but she just hasn't been the same since the skipper got roaring drunk one night and cut the links to its main memory banks."

"Did he have a reason?"

"He wanted to swap out most of the useful programs in favor of cheap porn interactives. He's a lonely, pathetic man."

"And this doesn't bother you?"

"Not too much, now. It only really affects the Ship's conscious AI. Backup dumb systems do most of the real work. I've learned to deal."

"That what a mate does, then, learn to deal?"

"Damn straight."

"Well, then, yeah," I said, squeezing the last of the milk out of the pack, "sounds like we have exactly the same job."

Prodamey called me up to the aft observation deck on the underside of the tug at six-hundred ship's time. She hadn't woken me up–the Sleepy Beddy Time milk had succeeded only in making my stomach churn to a different, more jazzy rhythm and my ears ring after the initial rush, not in allowing me to sleep. I had hoped to find Prodamey in as bad a shape as I was, but no such luck. She wasn't in the least disheveled. Of course, I'd been doing all her work the past few days.

"Sleep well?" I floated up next to her and strapped myself to the padded ceiling. The floor was transparent, an upside-down dome. Through it were the stars, the universe. If I'd been fully rested, I might have been impressed.

She nodded. "Best sleep I've had in a month. It's so quiet, so peaceful out here." She was looking out the dome but I don't think she was actually looking at the stars. "I should get one of these ships for myself. I think I'll buy one to celebrate my first director credit."

Back in Africa, she'd gotten word her agent–an AI, all she could afford at this point in her career–was on the verge of getting her the helm of the third remake of Pulp Fiction. "You've heard, then? Are congratulations in order?"

"The deal fell through."

"Sorry."

"Don't be." She didn't sound disappointed. Like she'd expected it and had prepared herself. "They're going with an AI. Tarantino's estate had one put together special for it. Supposed to replicate his thought process at ninety-three percent efficiency."

"Tough break."

"Studio politics." She shrugged. "Doesn't matter. This gig'll show 'em what I'm capable of. They'll have to give me a movie of my own after they see the footage we're doing for this piece of crap."

"Trees and a moon, those are gonna get you your own movie?"

"Artistic trees and moon. You saw the dailies of the trees. You can't tell me they weren't impressive."

I could. I mean, they were just trees, and Prodamey, truth be told, wasn't exactly what I'd call a talented director. Hell, she was only a marginally technically skilled one. She had the creative eye of one of those deep-sea eels—the basically blind kind. But she had an ego and a force of personality that had let her claw her way up from producing voice-chip work for pachinko machines to doing second unit directing for a major studio. In Hollywood, you could make do without talent and skill, but you wouldn't survive a three hour lunch meeting without an ego.

"Impressive enough," I said. No need to risk bruising that ego of hers. She could make my job hell.

"Which is why," she said, turning to stare at me with unsettlingly bright blue eyes, "nothing can go wrong with this shoot. Nothing."

Looking into her calculating yet stunning eyes I could understand, if only for a few seconds before I remembered just who I was dealing with, how she ended up getting her way so often. "Nothing will. It'll run smooth, you'll see."

"It had better. It's make or break time for my career, here, Charlie." She paused, turned to look out the dome. The dome was now glowing with a faint green light that extended a few centimeters away from the ship. We must have been coming up on the right location in the Lagrange point for the tug's wormhole generator to come online. "More than that, it's make or break time for your life. Understand?"

I didn't believe for a moment she'd made an actual threat against my life. Dramatics, that's all it was. But the real implication behind it was clear: my career would be over before hers, she'd see to that, if something went wrong. Union or not, she could probably swing insuring I never worked in Hollywood again. Maybe not even in India, Hong Kong, or Moscow.

I made a valiant attempt to be nonchalant. It came out sounding like I was a first-year drama student auditioning for the role of cowed underling. "You've got nothing to worry about. The platform's ready for action. You step into the booth, there'll be nothing stopping you from taking the best damned pictures of a moon ever set to digital storage."

"Good." She smiled. "You take care of the platform, I'll take care of the skipper."

"Why does the skipper need taking care of?"

"Call it a pre-emptive strike. Need to get him on our team, completely. Just in case. You never know. Same with the mate. Think you can handle her?"

"Handle her?"

"Yes, handle her. You're a good-looking enough guy. You're not exactly charming, but I imagine she doesn't get many prospects in her line of work, so doubt she'll be picky..."

"Wait... what? You want me to seduce her?"

"You can do that for us—for the film—right, Charlie? Or do I have to do everything?"

"Why do we need to seduce anybody?"

"Like I said, just in case. We're out here all alone, Charlie, trying to make Art. I'm not going to let a couple of teamsters compromise my vision."

"Who says they're gonna?"

"Things happen. I can't take chances here.–Look, I think it's starting."

The green glow outside had grown stronger. I was trying to focus on it, to get some feel for how far it extended, when all of a sudden it went away. I thought something had gone wrong–I expected sirens to go off again. Siren happy, I guess. But nothing happened. For a few minutes. We hung there on the wall in silence, waiting.

When the moment came, I just about missed it. Over before it began. A flash of non-light and the stars outside the dome were different. In all the wrong places. And good old Luna was gone. Where it had been was now just more blackness spotted with thousands of pricks of starlight, and one brighter star which was the gas giant around which the moon we were there to film was orbiting.

The moment of transition through the artificial wormhole had been briefer than my mind could perceive, a millionth of a millionth of a millionth second, or something even more unreal. I could almost convince myself I'd actually felt that incredibly brief moment–felt my body, the universe cease to exist–but of course that was just my feeble human mind trying to cope with the reality of it, trying to force a framework around the fact everything I was and ever knew had, if only for the briefest slice of time, stopped existing. Not physically unsettling, but something my mind would have trouble, and possibly even a little fun, integrating into its life experience model as time went by. Almost worth the inconvenience of zero-gee I'd been putting up with. You don't get that many paradigm shifts making movies. Well, not Hollywood movies, anyway.

I wanted the quiet in the observation bubble to last as long as possible. Prodamey had other ideas.

"That was it?" she asked, lighting a cigarette. "Mankind's greatest scientific achievement and that's all there is to it? Much ado about nothing, you ask me."

"You just don't get it."

"Oh, I get it. Science has no sense of art. Of showmanship. You show that flash to an audience, they won't know what happened. Talk about dead screen time."

I shook my head but didn't say anything. She was still my boss.

"Well," came the skipper's voice from the hatchway, "we're all squared away. Welcome to the Carden system." He looked past me, talked directly at Prodamey. Her back was to him but that didn't seem to matter.

As she turned to look back at him, she winked at me. "Thank you, Skipper. Now that we're here, I wonder if you could spare a moment to give me a tour of your wonderful ship? I've always been fascinated by space travel–especially wormholes. Could I see the wormhole generator, perhaps?"

The skipper blushed. "My ship, and everything aboard, is at your disposal." Unbelievable. Prodamey's charms looked to be working their dubious magic once more. Just like the safari leader during our shoot in South Africa. She'd gotten that particular sucker to use his own funds to fly in nine-course French meals from Cairo, just for her. My mind raced at what she'd end up getting the skipper to do for her.

They floated away for their tour. I stayed in the dome for a few more minutes, watching the stars.

It took me four hours to get the platform ready for duty, all by remote control from a waldo pod in the tug's small cargo bay. Directing repair and service robots by virtual reality, I made sure all the cameras worked, had their full range of movement, and were still wired up to the platform computers.

The platform had thirty cameras spread across its flat surface, top and bottom, leaving no blind spots and multiple camera over-laps except on the edges. Some were general purpose visible-light with adaptive lenses for any kind of zoom or focus Prodamey might need. Others were low-light models or were designed to film action scenes–to pick out details when what it was filming was moving too fast for the human eye. There were even a couple of infra-red jobs and a special camera with a nano-engineered lens for in-camera special effects. Almost thirty million dollars of studio money in that platform, and here they'd let me take it out for a spin. I only had to sign about a thousand pages of small-print to do it.

Once the platform was squared away, I went to fetch Prodamey. Found her in her cabin. Horror of horrors, the skipper was just leaving, fumbling with the buttons of his shirt and smiling all broad and proud as I passed him in the corridor.

Prodamey answered the hatch fairly quickly. She was dressed in sweats and arranging her hair. "Please, boss," I said, "tell me that wasn't what I thought it was."

"Turns out sex in zero-gee is less interesting than I imagined it would be."

"I'll keep that in mind." Actually I wouldn't. I planned to actively forget it as soon as I could. "The platform's ready. You ready?"

"Let's go."

She followed me out into the hall and down to the cargo bay. On the way, she asked: "Any luck with the mate yet?"

"Haven't run into her since we got into the system, but never fear," I said, mustering as much false self-confidence as I could, "we'll be rutting like wild animals before the end of the trip."

"Good. You're doing a fine job, Charlie. Keep it up."

The mate stuck her head into my cabin and found me in my sleeping bag, just at the brink of sleep. After buttoning up the platform following nine hours of Prodamey filming the moon–nine hours of crap that we'd need to reshoot tomorrow because the gas giant had been in the wrong place, according to Prodamey–my body was finally ready for a decent sleep. Should have known that wasn't going to happen.

"Remember how you said you're basically a glorified gopher?" she asked.

"Yeah," I said, apprehensive.

"Well, time to do some gophering."

"Huh?"

"Come on. I need a hand."

"Doing what?"

"Ever worn an EVA suit before?"

"No. And I don't think I want to."

"No sense of adventure."

"I just want to go to sleep."

"And that's exactly what you'll be able to do, once we run this little errand. Or don't you want to find out what your studio has gone to a whole lot of trouble and expense to send all the way out here?"

"Huh?"

"A message pod just popped into the system. It says it's for you." She smiled. "Of course, if you don't want it, I can tell it to go back home."

I unzipped the bag, tumbled out of it. "Lead the way."

The EVA suit was skintight, made up of several dozen layers of material, each layer having a different, important function. As the mate explained while she walked me through the spray-application process outside the dorsal airlock, the inner layers were life support, while the outer layers were designed to protect me from the void. One layer, densely filled with micro-channel conduits like a computer-designed sponge, shuffled sweat to the recycling system. Another used contracting and expanding ultra-strong ligaments to provide me with a whole new set of muscles, increasing my strength by a couple of factors. Yet another was designed to reflect all but enough radiation to keep my temperature comfortable, without freezing or frying me.

None of which made up for the discomfort of the application process. Like having hot wax sprayed over you by a pack of horny robot cats. And don't ask how I know what that feels like.

I had to wait inside the airlock for a few minutes while the mate suited up. Somebody had hung a battered teddy bear on the wall. Odd thing to find in an airlock. I asked the mate about it when she joined me.

"That's just Case," she said, her voice sounding slightly deeper over the suit-to-suit radio. "Had him since I was seven."

"Good luck charm?"

She hit a sequence of buttons on a control pad and air started to leak out of the lock. "Sort of. Watch."

The bear began expanding, getting bigger. By the time I couldn't hear the air being sucked away any longer, the bear was twice its original size.

"The lock's pressure sensor is out." She hit another button to cycle the external hatch. "Old Case there, he's a pretty good substitute. Foam insides, real loose stitching. Puffs up when there's no air pressure."

"Handy." I was looking at her instead of the blackness that was being revealed as the hatch drew open. When she slipped through the hatchway into the void, my eyes didn't follow her. They stayed locked on the wall.

"You coming?" she asked.

I forced my eyes away from the wall and got my first look at raw space, framed in the hatchway. It went on forever. Crystal clear blackness with a faint mist of stars spread across it. To my surprise, I didn't freak. I didn't get butterflies in my stomach, either. I just smiled. "Too neat."

"Has that effect on most. Get over it, and get out here. Need some help with this."

I stuck my head through the hatchway. Just outside the hatch, the mate was detaching a bulky cylinder cocooned in a framework of interlocking pipes. "And that that is?"

"A sled. Didn't think we were walking, did you?"

She had me loop my arm through a strap on the framework, then via her suit radio asked the ship's computer to activate the sled and transfer control of it to her suit's waldo systems. After she explained the whole concept of the sled to the ship, it did as she asked, and we jetted away from the tug on an invisible ion thrust.

"The pod came in to the system about an hour ago," she said, making minute, ghostly movements in her suit to control the trajectory of the sled. "It's been heading towards us since. We'll meet it half way."

"How long?"

"Ten minutes, at the most."

I shifted, spinning so my back was to the sled. The void was all around me now. Amazing. I could have spent hours staring into space, just existing, feeling myself a part of the universe. Not worrying about anything, fretting over work or Prodamey. But a memory of Prodamey's voice put an end to that. She'd wanted me to make special friends with the mate. Who knew why—I refused to understand the woman—but she was the boss. And besides, the mate was cute, in a rough, athletic, independent sort of way. Worth a try, even if my seduction skills weren't what I'd classify as anywhere near leading-man caliber.

"It's great out here, isn't it?" I said. It was the least lame thing I could think of to say.

"I suppose," she replied, quietly.

"A little jaded, are we?"

"No, just enjoying the nice, quiet ride."

And that was the end of my seduction of the mate.

I went back to letting space engulf me. Almost nodded off a few times. It was so peaceful, and I was so tired.

A proximity beeper went off in my suit when we were only a few hundred meters from the message pod. The mate stopped the sled with a blast of retros, then spun it to point it back towards the tug. As the pod passed us, the mate started up the sled's rocket again, matching speeds with the torpedo-shaped automated craft so we flew a meter beside it.

"It's asking for confirmation it's in the right place," the mate said. I couldn't hear the conversation she was having with the pod, relayed through the tug. She hadn't seen fit to put me in the loop, or maybe my suit wasn't equipped as well as hers. "The tug is... just confusing it."

"Understandable. Can I talk to it?"

"Sure. Just talk to me, my suit'll pass it to the tug, the tug will pass it to the pod. Hopefully the pod'll be able to set up its own radio link direct with your suit after that. Or else we'll have to relay its answers back through the tug and me."

"Let's hope.–Hello, message pod," I said.

The pod must have had enough artificial intelligence to recognize my voice as an authorized representative of the studio. It negotiated with my suit's radio for a secure frequency, then revealed the contents of its message in a short burst of encryption. My suit translated.

"Aww, shit," was all I could say after hearing it.

"What is it?"

I shook my head. "Trouble."

"What kind of trouble?"

"The big, hoary kind. Script changes. God, I hate re-writes."

───────────────

Prodamey met me in the editing suite aboard the platform once we brought the pod back and downloaded its contents. The script, along with panels containing producer and director notes, storyboards, and miscellaneous information, was holographically spread out around the suite. Prodamey took control of the remote.

"What's this part?" She scrolled the storyboard slowly through a sequence of quick-cut fire streaked clouds, shot from a dozen different angles.

"Oh," I said, reading the notes on the sequence on another panel. "That's a new bit for the end of the dream sequence. Instead of ending with the moon flyby, now it's going to end with Jackie burning up during re-entry into the planet's atmosphere."

Her face went pinched. "That's going to be tricky to shoot."

"Don't need to shoot it. Says here they're going to do it with CGI back at the studio. These are the pre-vizes. They don't look half bad."

"Then what are we supposed to be filming out here?"

"They wouldn't mind some gas giant shots for FX reference, but after that... nothing. We get to go home."

"What?" The pinch transformed itself into righteous indignation. "Don't they think I can handle it?"

"I don't think anyone could handle it. Re-entry would be a complicated shot. Dangerous. We'd have to bring the whole platform into the atmosphere. The tug, too. Way too complicated, way too risky."

"But it could be done?"

"We'd burn up the platform and the tug."

"Maybe."

"Probably." I shrugged. "The whole thing's moot anyway. I doubt the skipper would even let us try."

"Oh," she said, smiling. "He'll let us try. I told you I'd take care of him."

She was serious. That look in her eyes told me arguing with her wouldn't change her mind. My only hope was that the skipper would show some heretofore unseen strength of character and turn her down, and if he didn't, I'd have enough strength of character myself to refuse to help her, and even try to stop her.

My hopes and prayers were with the skipper.

———————

"The skipper's gone insane."

I was drinking lunch in the galley, scanning through the new script. They'd made a lot of changes, not just with the dream sequence our moon shots were originally a part of. They'd tacked a totally incoherent happy ending on to it. So much for sticking to the source material–Camus must have been spinning in his grave, but that's what you get when you put a Jackie Chan simulacrum in "The Stranger" and let comedy writers have a go at it. Prodamey had told me to work out the details of sending the platform down into the atmosphere to simulate re-entry. I hadn't bothered, confident the skipper wouldn't volunteer for a suicide mission.

"Completely insane," the mate continued her rant as she thrust herself into the galley. She slapped the baggie of hamburger and fries from my hands. It spun across the cabin, bounced off the wall with a wet thump.

"What was that for?" I asked, wiping my mouth.

"That was for letting your boss convince my boss that this tug can survive an atmosphere entry."

"Don't tell me the skipper's going along with her?"

She nodded. "Yeah, they're both insane. And it's all your fault."

"Oh, no it's not. I told her we'd probably all die."

"Not probably. Definitely. This tug isn't built for atmosphere work. It's about as streamlined as a block of wood. And we'll burn up just as easily. Why the hell didn't you tell me she was thinking about this?"

"I didn't... the skipper's not a strong man, is he?"

"This was her plan all along, wasn't it? You knew, since you came on board, and you didn't even bother to mention it. What, do you two have some kind of weird suicide pact?"

I shook my head. "I didn't know. Neither of us did. That pod had script changes, remember? The shots Prodamey wants to do in the atmosphere are new shots the studio is going to generate in a computer back home. She thinks she can do them better, live."

"She's insane, too."

"No argument here."

"So you're going to help me stop her?"

"Yeah, of course," I said. "But logic and reason won't work—her mind's set on doing this."

"And she's got the skipper convinced they're the reincarnations of Cleopatra and Anthony, or at least Ozzie and Harriet. I've never seen him so bad, so compliant."

"Then we'll have to do something physical."

"If the ship could be convinced it's in danger, it might let us cut off the skipper's command authorization," she said.

"Let's do that, then. We show the ship the flight plan, it's bound to recognize the inherent danger."

"Right... Ship?"

"What do you want now?" Ship replied over the intercom after a couple seconds. It sounded perturbed.

The mate pursed her lips. "Access the navigation system. The skipper just filed a new route. Run it through the simulator and tell me how it turns out."

"Can't we do this later? I was just having the simulator run World War II over again, only with snow globes instead of machine guns. Should be interesting to see what happens, don't you think?"

"I don't care. Run my request now. Time is of the essence here, Ship."

"Isn't it always with you people? Why don't you just speed up your internal clocks and give yourself some extra cycles to play with?"

"Just run the route simulation, will you?" the mate asked.

"The what? What are you talking about? Who are you, anyway? Is this another trick? Look, I told you people last time I am not interested in selling bulk food at warehouse prices to my friends and family."

"Ship, that'll be all for now," I said, interrupting. Then, to the mate: "This is getting us nowhere. Any way we can sabotage the engines? Take them out temporarily, buy us some time?"

"Sure, but anything we can do to the ship, the skipper can have the repair systems fix. Unless we do some real damage, but then we'd be stuck out here forever."

"Any time we can buy ourselves is time to maybe get the skipper to come to his senses. Or have a heart attack or something."

She shrugged. "Right. To the engine room, then."

While we were pulling ourselves along the long hallway to the engine room, we suddenly felt gravity. It was only a small physical tug, less than a tenth gee, but it could only have meant one thing. We were heading for the planet.

Prodamey's voice came over the ship's public address system. "Charlie, where the heck are you? Be a dear and board the platform. I can run it myself remotely, but I think this kind of a shot really deserves someone being about the platform, to give it some real authenticity."

I kept on pulling myself along the rail, following the mate. "We don't need to do the atmosphere shots," I yelled so the intercom could hear me. I assumed it would relay the message. "They're doing them back home."

"But we can do them live. CGI always looks like crap, no matter how much money they throw at it. I—we—will be taking the shots that can save this picture. We'll be heroes."

"We'll be dead," I said. The mate went down at a junction. I scooted after her into the semi-circular, spottily lit engine room. "You want to take those shots, you're on your own. I quit."

The mate smiled back at me. I wondered if she thought my expression was one of stern resolve, which is what I wanted her to think, or simple fear and confusion, which it actually was now that I'd very likely thrown my show biz career down the proverbial toilette.

"Fine," Prodamey said, after a pause. There was a definite edge of betrayal in her voice. "You'll never work in films again, you know that?"

"Yeah, I guess I do," I said back. The mate was floating over a control panel. "--How's it look?"

She shook her head, spoke low so her voice couldn't be picked up. "Bad as I expected. The skipper actually remembered to lock out these auxiliary controls. We're not stopping this any easy way."

"Well, then, just get me a wrench and tell me where to start smashing equipment."

"It's not that simple." She pointed at the display. "The most we could hope for with sabotage is to shut down the engines, but if we shut down the engines now, we'll still be headed straight for the planet with no way to adjust our trajectory."

"When you say 'straight for' you mean 'into', right?"

She nodded. "We're screwed."

"There must be something we can do."

"Nothing. Just hang out and wait for the atmosphere proximity alarm to go off. Shouldn't take long after that until we find out how it feels to be a pot roast."

Alarm. That got me thinking about sirens. And that got me thinking about: "Wait a second–the other day, you said the re-possession system has its own real-space and worm-hole drives."

Her face lit up. "Its own control systems, too."

"How can we get to them?"

"We can't. I mean, it's all isolated from the normal ship systems. For obvious reasons."

"There's got to be a way to hack it."

"Trust me. It's been tried, a couple thousand times, by real hackers, never with any success. The bank repossession systems are more secure than most planetary military systems. No way in, otherwise everybody would just keep turning their clocks back so it never knows a payment's been missed."

I smiled. "Sure, no way in if you want to set the clock back, but how much effort you think the bank put into keeping people from setting the clock forward?"

"Less?"

"I bet way less."

She smiled back. "That might work.–Ship!"

"What?" Ship whined. "You know there's a planet headed for us? It's very pretty."

"I'm sure," she said. "Ship, what is the date?"

"How the hell should I know?"

"Open your utility sub-system and repeat after me. The year is now 24-85, common era."

"If you insist. The year is now 24-85, common era. New date recorded. Oh, how the time flies."

The mate and I looked at each other. Nothing was happening. The mate sighed. "The re-possession system must has its own clock. Damn it. Been nice working with you, Charlie."

"Warning," announced Ship, in a different voice. "Uragon-Marshall Corporate has not received a regularly schedule mortgage payment on this vessel in the last three-hundred and fifty years. Self-re-possession will begin immediately. Please be advised that upon arrival at Lunar Fields dry-dock, this vessel will be impounded and the credit rating of all parties to the mortgage will be flagged for civil and criminal investigation."

I glanced at the mate. "Your five percent..."

The mate shrugged. "That I can live with."

The light gravity in the tug went away, and a few seconds later was replaced with a much stronger pull, this one from a slightly different angle, as if the ship was also slowly turning. Turning back towards the Lagrange point.

It took them two months to sort out what had happened, once the bank and the studio got their lawyers involved.

The skipper agreed to retire. He'd been planning on it, anyway, and it was that or face charges from the Shipping Commission.

The mate got the tug ship. And a healthy retainer from the studio to never talk publicly about the incident.

Prodamey got herself fired. Blackballed, too. I hear she's trying to make a new start of it back in commercial production in Neo-Communist China.

Me, I sold a spec script on the whole affair to a rival studio. They're getting the AI Tarantino to direct it, and they figure it'll be big, if only I make some slight changes. Like adding some alien pirates, an exploding star, and a pack of space-dwelling giant tiger sharks. Shit, for the kind of money they're offering, I'd even take out the steamy sex scene between me and the mate. But that they like.

They offered me the second unit on the film.

Yeah, I passed.

Seven

DISSECTING HENRIES

THE BODY ON THE cot is familiar. A little younger. The skin is in better condition, seen a lot less wear and tear. The muscle tone is better, too, a lot more defined. The speedigrow process is responsible for that. But there's no mistaking who it is.

It's Henry.

Henry clone. Void of consciousness, so they say, big parts of its brain missing. Engineered out of the equation. Just enough stem and cerebellum in there to keep the heart beating, the lungs taking in air. Not enough to let the eyes see, but they still dart around, random and blind.

Original Henry is standing over clone Henry. Been hovering and staring, examining every pore, every hair, every part of this other self for the better part of a day. Studying.

Time to start, Henry tells himself, plucking the largest scalpel from the tray of instruments at the head of the cot. Surgical steel, room-temperature. Not exactly sanitized but there's no need for it.

Henry has set mirrors up against the walls of this room so he can look up from time to time and catch himself standing over himself, scalpel in hand. He looks up now and the rush is indescribable. Exactly what he's seeking. The rush. However many times it flows over him, its effect is as strong as that first time a year ago, the moment his obsession was sparked.

He makes then first cut, drawing down from the shoulders to the sternum, then down from there past the navel, like he learned how to do from a supernet autopsy site.

The clone's eyes stop moving randomly. They flash downward, trying to see what's happening in its chest, a strange, curious expression on its face.

The clone doesn't make a noise, though. Its body is awash with nanchines of Henry's own design that block most all pain at the nerves before they are transmitted up the synapse chain. He left some pain in. Not out of cruelty, but to be fair to the clone. Even with its less-than-animal consciousness the clone deserves to have some sense of what is happening to it. Henry imagines the feeling of the scalpel in the nanchine-induced semi-numbness as something not unpleasant, more akin to the feeling of a finger traversing the skin. Slow, sensual. Loving. Maybe he'll try it himself someday.

Henry has decided to concentrate on the abdomen with this clone. The liver, the intestines, the colon, all of the low-profile stuff that never gets good press. He's watched a beating heart often enough, time for something different. He reminds himself to take care not to accidentally cut open the stomach.

Henry draws back skin, cuts through muscle. His bare hands get messy, a child playing in the mud. He'll go at it like this for hours.

He glances up at the clone's face and there it is. The smile. The clone is smiling. A simple reaction to the numbed-down sensations of having its body shredded, interpreting them as pleasure? Or is it something deeper, something hidden to Henry's present understanding and ability to sympathize, as death comes closer? Of all the mysteries, the questions he obsesses over, this is the one that fascinates and frightens Henry the most.

Why do they always smile?

"I need another one."

"Just got you one."

"And I appreciate it. But I need another one."

"What the fuck you do with them, anyway?" Jackie asks, sitting across from Henry in the cramped, straight-backed, bare wood booth in the back of the Kast. She's idly carving random gouges in the table with a fork, adding her own designs to the layers left behind by countless patrons going back a century if the bartender's tales are to be believed. "Been going through them like potato chips. They are made to last awhile--couple years at least before rapid cell de-gen sets in. You stocking up? Building your own little army?"

"You know, that's the first time you've asked me that. I'm not exactly comfortable with the question, okay?"

"Well, get comfortable with it. I'm tired of playing the blind procurer here."

Henry decides it's time to change the subject with something that always manages to distract Jackie. Her own obsession. "I've managed to push the upper range of the nans. Had to re-engineer the control unit to go up to eleven, know what I'm saying?"

Jackie's face lights up. "Seriously?"

"Always."

"Look, we shouldn't even be meeting out in the open like this."

"Who the fuck's gonna see us?"

"You kidding? It's fuckin' Renaissance week. The place is crawling with tourists. Besides, there's Heathers everywhere." She points at three teens sitting at the bar, dressed all in black like TV ninjas, 3D high-def cameras surgically anchored onto the right side of their skulls. They aren't talking to each other. Just slowly spinning around on their bar stools, different rotation rates, their cameras taking it all in. Transmitting the scene real-time back to a supernet distribution node for the benefit of the world, or at least whoever's tuned in at the moment.

"Forget them. Probably some local cult show with all of a dozen viewers. Global nets wouldn't bother with our little bar, not with the big show going on at the Cathedral tonight."

"Local's what I'm worried about. If anyone from the lab sees me..."

"Sees you doing what? Having a drink with an old friend?" Henry asks, pointedly ignoring the fact he's got no drink in front of him, doesn't intend to have one and Jackie knows it. "Shit, this is Pittsburgh. Nothing we're doing is illegal here."

"Who gives a fuck about illegal? Someone sees us and starts asking questions, I could end up losing a lot more than my job. Find out I'm using the tubs for 'non-job related activities' and I'm history. They don't like that kind of shit."

"So, they fire you. You come work for me, then. Get you all the equipment you need."

"You're not listening to the subtext here, are you?" She wrinkles up her forehead.

"I'm listening."

"Just don't care, do you?"

"Not my concern, right now, sorry. Got other things I gotta worry about. So, do you want the new nans or not?"

"Yeah, yeah. Of course. How much and when?"

"Growing about three gallons worth as we speak. Be done in the morning."

"I'll swing by."

"Nah, not ready. Have to tweak the control units, right?"

She nods, disappointment in her heart-shaped, almond-eyed face. A face Henry once thought he loved. "So, when?" she asks.

"I'll have three dozen done by the end of the week. Saturday at the latest. Can you have my thing for me by then?"

"Maybe. I'm working graveyard Thursday. Don't think the speed-igrow tubs are booked. Wouldn't happen to have brought a sampler?"

Of course he did. Knows Jackie better than he knows himself. Knows what drives her, why she smiles. A simple, uncomplicated buzz will do the trick, every time. The purer the better. She keeps half the shit he trades her for the clones instead of selling it like she should be doing, making herself some big cash, buying her way out of town and Out West where she's got family and maybe a future. But that isn't her dream. Was, once, back in pre-history. She has other goals now.

If only his own goal was so transparent. He might not have to bother with the clones. After all, it is a search for his true self, he likes to believe, that keeps him doing what he does, all alone, the two of him, in his mirrored room. Looking for reasons, a measure of his identity somewhere in the viscera of his own body. He isn't entirely sure what he'd do if he found it. He suspects he'd truly miss the rush, if he stopped.

Henry smiles and pulls a vintage Walkman from his jacket pocket. The tape deck is simply a shell. He cracks it open, dumps its contents out on the table before her. A vial of clear liquid and a plastic stick with two sliding levers. She takes the vial, untwists the top. Drinks the contents down.

"New suspension?" she asks, wincing.

"Threw some licorice in, for variety."

"Fuckin' awful."

"Noted." Henry points at the control stick. "Give it a try."

"Don't they need to settle in? Always need to settle in."

"Not anymore. Fixed that. They spread a lot faster now. Thirty second dispersion someone your weight and height."

She gives him an unbelieving look but still reaches for the stick. "Haven't screwed with the controls, right? Left is still frequency, right volume?"

"Check. Only adjusted the volume levels."

Jackie thumbs both levers up at the same time. He watches her hand, sees it start to tremble, then looks up at her face. This is a familiar buzz for her, comfortable. The nanchines have sought out nerve endings throughout her body, attached themselves. Now getting radio signals from the stick to pulse the nerves, fool them into transmitting up to Jackie's mind that the most pleasurable thing in the universe is happening to her.

Not as pleasurable as possible, though.

She smiles at him. Then pushes the levers all the way up.

The stick drops from her suddenly convulsing hand. She's blissed. Slack, stupid grin on her face, head rolling. She grabs the edges of the table with both hands, her body moving in quick little shivers of pleasure, looking like she's barely able to stop herself from bursting. Nobody in the bar gives her a second look, not even the Heathers. It's Pittsburgh, after all.

Henry is pleased with himself. Used to do this kind of thing for a real living, programming and designing pharmaceutical nanchines. It's not a career anymore, but only odd jobs, contract stuff and the pleasure nans–for Jackie and a few actual low-level street dealers. It earns him enough to pay the rent and feed himself, and provides for his singular, very expensive hobby.

Henry takes the control, throttles Jackie back to a tenth power.

"Eleven is good," she says, out of breath.

"Glad to know." He never uses his own nans. Doesn't trust the little fuckers running around in his body. "So, this weekend, then?"

"Yeah. You know, Henry," Jackie says, trying to collect herself, "you don't have to go home alone, always."

He slips the empty tape deck back in his pocket, quickly slides out of the booth. "Yeah, yeah I do."

———————————

Pittsburgh is dressed up like a John Waters version of the 16th Century, as if daVinci's sensibilities had run towards the white-trash end of the spectrum and the Medicis had hired him to drape the whole of Florence in pink chiffon and ribbons of gold lamé.

The whole Renaissance Faire Week is the Pittsburgh Autonomy council's idea to get tourists into the city during the slow late winter months, let local merchants wring a couple extra bucks out of the suckers of the world. The town fills with idiots dressed up in period costume, wandering around the made-up downtown goggling sword jugglers and mud-people street theater. About as much to do with the real Renaissance as TV and real life.

Natives like Henry could live their whole lives without the whole scene. Pittsburgh is weird enough all the time, with its Heather gangs, windowsill snipers, thriving drug and sex trade, never-close rave churches, and violent crime rate highest in what is left of the country.

Setting aside a special time of year for it to let loose strikes Henry as superfluous, not to mention annoying.

But anything which disrupts his routine he finds annoying.

He usually walks home past the Cathedral of Knowledge, in the park, relatively safe on its well-lit cobblestone paths, but there's a gathering there tonight, a performance on high-wire, some kind of circus and history lesson combined. Crowds way too thick to wade through if he wants to make it home before dawn.

Henry takes the long way around, up behind the old Masonic temple and the dark maze of alleys spreading out behind its imposing facade. Glad he's wearing his city survival gear—jeans, tee and a German-made, Kevlar-lined overcoat with borderline-fashionable balloon lapels and semi-rigid, transparent hood, also bulletproof. Doesn't trust the Masons. Doesn't know why—probably race memory, he muses.

Because of the Faire, Henry is not alone in the alley. A steady stream of traffic clusters walk it, in both directions. Henry ends up pacing one of the clusters, a mixed group of natives and tourists, even some Heathers.

And one woman walking alone about thirty yards ahead, outside the comfortable confines of even a group of strangers simply walking the same way and speed as she. Older woman, wearing a bright neon fanny pack. Idiot, Henry thinks, wondering how long it'll be until the predators descend.

Not long at all.

Traffic flows to a halt, organic, Henry one of the first to stop. Something in the shadows, or the women's nervous glance at an unnatural pile of empty cardboard boxes to her left as she passes, keys everyone in.

The mugging is quick and painless. Painless for Henry, watching safely from within the crowd of curiosity seekers which has bunched around him. Nobody moves to interfere, to stop the thing.

The Heathers wouldn't, in any case, their whole kink recording whatever happens as it happens, simply observing, non-participation as art form.

The others in the crowd have their own reasons for hanging back, Henry knows. The locals, the Pittsburgh natives, they see the victim is a tourist and therefore doesn't count, and that the muggers–locals themselves–have a right to conduct their business without undue restrictions. The few tourists in the crowd, maybe they think it's street theater, or figure there for the grace of.

Henry's reason is a lot more basic. Scared to help.

So he watches with the rest, sees how the thing is almost a ritual for the three muggers, these kids with their heads hidden under old-fashioned riot helmets, otherwise naked except for long gold chains dangling from pierced scrotums, each taking quick, jerking stabs at the woman in turn with survivalist blades. She collapses immediately to the street under the assault.

They cut her fanny pack free and they're gone, down the street, laughing, howling.

Once they are out of earshot, the crowds disperse, shamble away to continue their search for other bright sparks of action to catch their fleeting attention.

Henry doesn't cut a wide path around the dead woman like the rest. Drawn, he steps close to her, cautious, curious.

He should head back home, fast as he can, it isn't safe here, even with his heavy bullet-proof overcoat. The muggers probably won't return themselves, but a scavenger gang might happen along, smelling the fresh kill and looking for anything valuable overlooked and left behind, or simply hungry for a fresh meal.

But then there is his obsession, and he finds he must, for whatever reasons his subconscious has, look down at the body. He will wait here and stare at the dead woman, let his mind pursue its tangents until something either connects and he can go home with a new insight, or the moment fizzles and he must return home under a cloud of depression, an opportunity lost.

After a minute, he gets the Idea.

Usually he'll spend the morning after an autopsy cleaning up, bagging the body for trash day, scrubbing the blood from the floor and mirrored walls. But now he thinks that is wasting what might be a potentially rich and fulfilling avenue for his obsession to travel.

He's never watched a body decompose.

He has four days until Jackie gets him a new clone. Should give the body plenty of time to get a good decay going, especially if he cranks up the heat in his apartment.

It'll be interesting, at the least, and then there's an off chance it will give him that crucial flash of insight into the whole clone-smiling-at-death's door enigma. He won't count on it, but it can't hurt to try.

He hurries off to his apartment, things to do.

A decomposing body is on the whole the least exciting thing in the universe to watch. Henry comes to that conclusion early on, but he sticks with it, just in case, sitting in his mirrored room on a lawn chair reading Kafka and sipping iced tea. He looks up at the body from time to time, ponders the meaning of it all, losing himself in thoughts of decay and the inevitable.

The mirrors reflect a dozen versions of himself. Both selves. Himself watching himself decompose, a dozen times over. The dizzying philosophical complexities bring a pensive smirk to his lips.

He's been watching the decay for four days, stopping only to make more tea and drifting to sleep as little as he could manage. Spent all his time in the mirrored room, blown off working the whole time. Hasn't made a single adjustment to a control stick, worse yet, he's not given the latest batch of nans proper attention and they've died in their vats.

Jackie'll be pissed. He'll make it up to her. He has more important things to do.

The knock at the front door startles him. Nothing worse than being startled when you're sitting in a room with a dead clone.

He recovers quickly, collects his thoughts and stands, feels a stiffness in his knees and wonders if he should concentrate on the next clone's legs.

The mirrored room shares a short hallway with the front door, a bed sheet curtain hanging in the room's doorframe. He takes care to close off the mirrored room from view of the hallway, draws the sheet tight across the doorframe and ties it at each corner and at the midpoints, secure. He checks each knotted shoelace twice before he throws a bathrobe over his scrubs and opens the front door.

Jackie is there, and she is not alone. She's got his new clone with her. It's wearing a baggy lab coat, shivering. The face is Henry's and partially hidden under a wide-brimmed, floppy hat with crocheted flowers sewn onto it.

Jackie's taken better care in dressing herself. She's tucked inside a full set of faux-denim body armor and a serious looking riot helmet. It is daytime, after all.

Henry plants himself squarely in the doorway. Jackie knows the routine. She shouldn't expect to be invited in.

"Morning," she says, and flicks the helmet's visor up. "Well, don't you look like crap? Forget to sleep the last couple days?"

"Caught a cold," Henry lies. "Knocked me around. Haven't been able to..."

"No new sticks?"

Henry shakes his head. "Worse than that. Made a mistake and killed the elevens."

She lets out a sigh. Exasperation. Henry gets the feeling she isn't surprised, sees she holds a control stick in her clenched fist, her thumb working the levers. "Great."

"Look, I'm really sorry."

"I suppose you still want me to give you clone-boy here, right?"

"If you don't mind."

"Where the fuck I gonna keep him, anyway? So, where are they?" Jackie asks, craning to look around him into the apartment.

"They who?"

"You know who. Your little army of Henries."

"There's no army."

"Okay, but you gotta have a dozen of them. Thirteen, now. Can't I see them?"

"I don't think that's a good idea."

"What, you dress 'em up or something?"

"No. Look, now's a bad time."

"Gotta live for the moment, Henry."

Before he can stop her, even consciously register what she is doing, Jackie ducks under his arm and steps around him. She is brandishing a pocket knife that she's pulled from somewhere, stabs it into the bed sheet curtain near the top, and draws it down. Slices the sheet wide.

A move, he senses from her stance as she looks past the shredded curtain and gently folds the knife away, she has been practicing in her mind for some time.

Still, she obviously hasn't prepared herself for what she sees. But how could she have anticipated this, Henry asks himself, feeling sorry for her more than embarrassed for himself.

He sees her face go paler, then sees her gag, fighting to hold back getting sick. He hasn't realized until this moment the smell in the room is on the overwhelming side. He's gotten used to it.

Henry leads her to the chair, picks it up and spins it around to face away from the decomposing clone. She sits at his urging. "I knew you were a little twisted," she says. "But I figured you were just fucking them."

"Nothing like that."

"Oh, yeah, this is much more socially acceptable. Why?"

"I don't know."

"Bullshit," she says. She twists around to steal a glance at the body. Snaps back around. "You do this for a reason. You gotta have a reason, right?"

"At first, I wanted to see. Curiosity. Since then, well, it's gotten... complex."

"Or maybe you're crazy. Christ, Henry."

"Look, Jackie, I'm sorry, but this is just something I do."

"Just something you do?"

"Yeah."

"Should've never gotten you that first one."

"In a way, best thing you ever did for me."

"Oh, don't lay this on me. This is it, man. No more."

"You can't cut me off. I'm close."

"Close to what?"

"I don't know," he answers, and it is the truth.

"Fine," she says, standing. She palms the control stick again and Henry sees her slide the levers two thirds the way up. "I'm outta here. And don't expect me back. Hope you enjoy this clone, 'cause he's your last."

Henry looks back at the still open front door. "Um, where is the clone?"

It's too bright outdoors. Henry stands on the stoop of his apartment, squints up and down the street. Should be easy enough to spot the clone. The lab coat and stupid hat should stand out in any crowd. But there's no crowd on the street. It's daytime. Pittsburgh is a night city, practically deserted during the day. Deserted for a reason.

It's a sport these days, everybody does it. Windowsill sniping. Young and old, a way to pass the time, they sit in a window with a high-powered rifle waiting to snipe at anybody foolish enough to wander by. Henry tries not to think about that as he stands out in the open. He'd feel better if he was wearing something a little more substantial than his scrubs and bathrobe. Like his Kevlar overcoat, but he's only going to be out here a second. Has to find the clone.

Jackie is checking the rest of the building while Henry checks the street. Henry found the apartment foyer wide open, and fears his clone has wandered out into the world.

Shit, the thing can't see, Henry reminds himself. It can't have gone far. On its own.

And no one is on the street. Good.

Unless the clone was instantly abducted by a passing motorist, the clone must still be inside. Jackie'll find it. No need to worry. He'll get the clone, experiment the weekend away, cook up a huge batch of nans to help patch things up with Jackie and keep the clones flowing.

He turns to go back in to the building and his spine shatters, at the base.

Swears he hears someone across the street laughing as he crumples down to the concrete steps. Sounds like old freak-man Yusalon.

Henry has never liked Yusalon, always trying to lure neighborhood kids into his third-floor apartment by throwing candy from his window with the promise of more for those brave and stupid enough to go up.

As he lay on the steps, for the moment, all Henry can think of is he ought to have a word with the old man about that. No way to behave.

Henry feels a dull thump, this time below his collarbone. He knows his body well enough to be certain both shots are fatal, especially that last one. He'll be dead in a few seconds.

He can't help smiling.

And at last he understands why.

Eight

THE ROAD TO SENILITY

GONNA MEET MY FATE with the sun at my back. Way I always wanted. Real-man kind'a shit.

I turn gentle cartwheels in slow terminal orbit, Jupiter's cold, beautiful bands of color filling my vision, and Mozart's Requiem as interpreted by a trio of ritual Japanese Shinto drummers beating mercilessly, sublimely at my eardrums.

The modified EVA mining suit doesn't allow me much freedom of movement, but don't need much to kill myself. All I need's a good view, a good sound system, and a moment to reflect, put everything into perspective.

Came to Jupiter to cap off my life. No fuss, no muss, no big deal. The logical thing to do. Been a good life. Had some fun, my share of women -- real and artificial. Personally brought down a government or two. Have a incorporeal kid who's taken over vast portions of the solar system's computer networks with an army of artificially intelligent virtual pets, made his pappy proud. Millions know my name, recognize my face. Granted, most of them want to put a bullet into it, but hey, fame isn't free.

Not sick or anything. Not physically. Worn and torn, sure, but with a technological assist I'd have a few good decades left in me.

So why? Tired, I guess. Life's lost its luster.

More than that, don't want to end up like Dave. Anything but that. Bottom line, I am one-hundred-and-two years old. That's enough. About time I got on with this.

Reach for the emergency purge valve. I made some alterations to it back on the charter trawler I'd hired to haul me out here, to override the safeties that usually prevent the escape systems from cracking the suit open when it doesn't sense atmosphere outside. Death may not be quick, but it will be interesting, which is far better, if you ask me.

Rest my hand on the valve, take a last look down at Jupiter. Familiar big red spot storm swirls and churns, lightning strands longer than Earth is wide flashing within. Watch as it slides off around the curve of the planet, smile at myself that something that big can move so fast. Glad I had a chance to see that.

Get a solid grip on the valve as down on Jupiter, another storm comes up over the curve. Little baby storm, can't be bigger than Luna. But it's size isn't what stops me from twisting the valve.

The way the light hits the storm, it looks like it could be a face. Not a pretty face. It's got horns sprouting from its cheeks and one-too few eyes.

Stare at it as it crawls its way around the lower hemisphere. Don't know how long I stare.

It's a sign. A miracle. A holy revelation like Dark Age peasants used to get after one too many slices of hallucinogenic-mold infested rye bread.

Yeah, right.

Miraculous sign my ancient, wrinkled ass. A coincidence of chaos, that's all, brought about by wind and storm and pure chance, like that face on Mars they turned into the theme park that once and for all bankrupted Disney.

But I can make money off this. There is something to live for, after all. Same thing there's always been -- profit.

Gingerly let go of the valve and turn the Mozart off with the tongue-switch. "Yo, Cap'n Bobby," I say, the suit's radio kicking on at the sound of my voice, "hope like hell you're listening. I've reconsidered the whole graceful suicide thing. Gonna need you to come back and pick me up. Before my ox runs out, if it's all the same to you."

Silence. If I were Cap'n Bobby I would have lit the engines and headed the fuck back to the Belt the second the airlock hatch cycled closed and the crazy old man left the trawler. Take the money and run, a philosophy that's never let me down. But not everybody lives by it, and besides, got another trusty philosophy: Always leave yourself an out. Even when planning to kill yourself.

I clear my throat. "If it helps you make up your mind, I can still cancel payment."

Static. Then: "Be there in fifteen."

Money wins the day yet again. Now, there's a sign for ya.

———

The Gerald Ford Memorial Long Term Care Residential Station at L5 has two things going for it, far as I can see. It doesn't spin on its short axis any faster than to give it half-a-gee grav max on the inside of its outermost hull -- extremely important as my muscle tone ain't what it used to be -- and more importantly, it's cheap, since somehow I let myself get talked into paying half of Dave's bill.

As if I didn't have enough reasons to resent the old bastard clinging so desperately to life.

Cap'n Bobby stays aboard the trawler while I go fetch Dave. Was easy to convince Bobby to go along -- he's a ship-for-hire after all, just had to convince him to wait until it's all done to get paid. Money'll be rolling in by that point. He bought it, my enthusiasm the clincher. Always is.

Robot pod leads me down through the station's uncomplicated corridors, walls painted with ever-changing relaxation-inducing patterns, past deck after deck of open wards disguised as oversized, communal living rooms. In the wards, the old and dying pretend they're leading useful lives of sitting around and watching each other drool, all the while waited on hand, foot, and automated wheelchair by robot nurses who never complain and never once inspire even the kinkiest of sexual thoughts, they're that utilitarian. No humans on staff. Work's too depressing.

I suppose there are worse ways to spend the waning years seniling away, but any question why I preferred the suicide route?

Dave's in one of the living room wards, playing holographic chess against the built-in computer set to kiddy level, and by the look, losing badly.

The years have not been as kind to him as to me. I can pass for fifty, still fit, trim and dashing. He'd have trouble passing for two-hundred. All those chemicals the nanochine factory in his belly has made for him over the years have taken their toll.

He's put on weight, but not enough to stretch the wrinkles out of his leathery skin or remove the gauntness from his sallow face. His left hand has the unmistakable jitter of onset Parkinson's and there are scars on his forearms where they yanked his pop-out gun implant and replaced it with packs of nerve dampeners to lessen the disease's symptoms. Got these big power-assist braces on his legs, can't walk by himself even in the half-gee of the station.

And worst of all, he's finally completely bald. Doesn't have the sense to have it regrown, either, he's that far gone.

He looks terrible, even for Dave. Worse than the last time I saw him, month or so ago, when I'd stopped by for one last visit before heading out to Jupiter and we got in to a World War IV-sized fight over some trivial thing that happened years ago -- me losing his life savings in a belt-based casino start-up (I was supposed to know the asteroid we'd bought a quarter of was Mormon controlled?) -- that ended in me doing a storm-out-of-the-room-fuck-you-pal routine.

I sit down across the board from him. Light up a cig, lean back. Haven't been able to smoke on the trawler, Cap'n Bobby's got this thing. I sit patiently, enjoy the cig. Let him speak first. If he has any sense, it'll be an apology.

"Oh, what the fuck do you want?" he asks, looking up from the board briefly after a minute of ignoring me. "Aren't you dead yet?"

Glad to see his fighting spirit is intact. "Something came up."

"Well, it can keep on going. I'm in the middle of something here." He drags a holographic pawn forward. The computer immediately captures it, puts him in check.

"Yeah, looks real engaging. You win you get an extra bowl of pablum for dinner?"

He shuts the chessboard down. "Again, I ask: what the fuck do you want?"

"Got a deal goin'. Come on, ship's waiting. Paying for it by the hour, so let's up and *imshi*, okay?"

"I'm not going anywhere with you," he says, almost whining.

"Of course you are. I'm rescuing you."

"I don't need rescuing. Told you before, I like it here."

"You only think you like it here," I say, passing him my cig. He takes it, sucks voraciously until a nurse swoops by and plucks it from his mouth. "That's what these places do. The mood music, the bland food, the programmed chameleon nanochine paint and it's happy-happy wall patterns, the robot nurses at your beck and call. They're all carefully designed to delude you into thinking you're content to while away your golden years in the stifling embrace of managed health care."

He sneers. "I've got four-thousand channels and the nurses let me putz around with their insides sometimes, if I don't make a fuss about my meds. Got most of them operating at one-and-a-half efficiency -- manuals said it couldn't be done. They got together and made me a plaque in appreciation."

Shake my head. He's a shell of the flake I once knew. Got to bring him around. "I need to remind you this wasn't your idea? When was the last time Rain and the kids came to visit? All that talk about this being the best for you, all bullshit. They just shoved you out here to keep you out of the way."

"They were up yesterday. Who do you think brought me the chess board, asshole?"

Oh. Light another cig while I think of something to say.

"Why are you trying so hard?" he asks.

"What?"

"For a third time: What the fuck do you want?"

"Told you."

"This deal is something you can't do without me? You never had such a high opinion of my abilities before."

"Not your abilities I need. It's your connections."

"I see. Need me to once again compensate for your complete lack of social skills and knack for offending everyone you've ever met?"

"Pretty much, yes. There's money in it."

Gets him thinking. He crunches his unibrow. Nothing he enjoys more than thinking there's something he can do I can't. This one time, he's right. "And I'm supposed to just drop everything and go with you, like old times? Forgive and forget?"

I blow smoke at him. "Exactly what 'everything' are you talking about?"

He looks around him and shrugs. "Fine. But you're not still on the suicide kick, are you?"

"Well, next stop's Earth orbit. You tell me."

––––––––––––

Maybe this wasn't such a good idea.

Dangerous being this close to a planet who's major governments -- what's left of them -- not to mention the majority of inhabitants want to see me die, the more horribly the better. In all honesty, I did do a number on them, a number of times, so can't blame them for their animosity. If Earth wasn't a third-class world, superseded by the economic and political powerhouses in the Belt and Mars, I might have worked to repair the relationship. But that and I didn't think I'd get any nearer to the old homeworld than Luna ever again since my last hasty departure, especially after killing myself, to make the effort worthwhile.

My presence here alone is likely to get Bobby's trawler boarded or simply blown into so much orbital debris if anyone discovers it. But that's not the bad idea I'm talking about -- that's purely the cost of business.

Bad idea was taking Dave along. One of those classic bad ideas, like invading Russia in the winter or that piece of crap seventh Star Trek series, the one with Mike Meyers and Jim Carrey as a Siamese-twin captain.

Thought I could put up with Dave for the sake of the deal. But is any amount of money worth this? Beginning to think not.

"They modified my stomach plant, the bastards," he informs me, for like the fiftieth time. "Populated it with nanochines that can only produce so-called beneficial drugs. Vitamins and shit. Can't dial up a good morphine-analogue hit or even nicotine-substitute anymore, damn bugs won't take my orders. Whenever I try they just squirt me extra vitamin C. No way to live, I tell you that."

He's been ranting the entire trip. I blame myself. Opened the floodgates by innocently asking him how he was doing. Thus began a non-stop litany of the aches and pains he must suffer indignantly daily, and the surgeries and nanochine body-mods he's endured to keep him alive one more day. Hardly seems worth it, to hear him complain. And that's all I've been doing. About had enough of it.

"Will you give it a rest?" I ask, letting my impatience get to me at last. "It's not like you're the only one age has been a bitch to, but you don't hear me complaining, do you?"

"Oh, like you've had any trouble at all." he says. "You don't look a day over ninety."

Over ninety? I look at him coldly. "Had to pull my rig out a couple months ago. Semi-bio components started rapid deterioration, my body began rejecting it as foreign." I hold up my left palm. Fine scar almost lost next to the thicker lifeline. I chuckle. "Believe that? In me since I was seventeen in one form or another and all of a sudden it's foreign."

"The whole rig?" he asks, waving at my head.

"Yeah."

His face goes all sad. For me. "I'm sorry. I didn't know."

"Yeah, well, it's no big thing. Okay?"

He looks at me like he knows it is a big thing, but he nods anyway.

"We've got signal," Cap'n Bobby announces over the ship's inter-com. "They're ready for you."

We'd been waiting for a call to go through to a neo-pagan-pro-to-cannibal community based in southern France. Very reclusive bunch of people -- more society's choice then their own -- and they won't talk to you unless they know you, and they don't know me. Why I needed Dave to do the contacting. Well, that and me being a wanted man in France. Unlike the rest of the planet, the French don't want me dead for the son I unleashed on the net, for wrecking the global economy twice, or for one of the dozen minor (and three major) wars I either started or finished -- no, they want me for despoiling the two things they love most, themselves and Jerry Lewis, by making a ten-hour time-tripping interactive-porn epic starring a computer generated, French-speaking Lewis playing a transvestite Joan of Arc. Sure, it won a boatload of Academy Awards, but the French, they just don't have any sense of humor.

I'm thankful for the interruption. The conversation was starting to get uncomfortably personal. Never should have brought him along.

―――――

We float into a makeshift holo-phone booth Cap'n Bobby's set up in the corner of the cramped secondary cargo bay and pull on garbage-bag hoods with small slits cut out for our eyes. Strap ourselves in to folding chairs bolted to the wall and hold bulky vocal-cord vi-brating voice disguisers up to our throats under the hoods as the phone comes online, filling the empty space in front of us with an image.

Image resolves into a man sitting at a table in what appears to be a typical French sidewalk café, but the lighting is all wrong for outside. A holo-phone set. The espresso cups on the table are empty, the bread plastic, the waiter in the background a life-sized cutout. The man is Hiram Liebneiz, leader of the neo-pagans and quite frankly a lunatic. He wears the full-on outfit of a sixteenth-century Venetian doge, and his hair is long and lacquered, twirled into three columns that practically double his height.

"Hiram," Dave says, "good to see you."

Hiram sits for a moment and stares. Wasn't expecting hooded men to be on the other end of the line. He balances a pair of thick-rimmed glasses on the tip of his nose, peers into the camera. "Dave? Is that you?"

"No names, please," I say. The disguiser makes me sound like Daffy Duck.

We have to take these precautions, speak through the disguisers and wear the hoods because I just don't trust the triple offset thousand-bit encryption we've got going on the phone channel. Supposed to be unbreakable, but I've heard reliable rumors that at least one second-generation quantum-based computer's been put into operation on the Earth's net, and if that's true, no encryption produced by a non-quantum system is safe anymore. And since our encryption ain't quantum, potentially the automated New United Nations anti-crime and terrorism scanning systems that sort through every bit of traffic in the net looking for keywords, vocal patterns, facial patterns, can spot me talking to the pagans and tag me for speedy follow-up by the governments with the active warrants for my death. So, rumor or not, I will wear the damn hood and have my voice sound like a cartoon character, no matter how much it makes me feel like a dork.

Dave isn't a wanted man himself -- escaped that distinction some-how, his vaunted people skills, no doubt -- but he's what they call a "known associate" of mine, and if they detect him, they're bound to leap to an inconvenient conclusion and at least send an interceptor to board us for a look see. That's what I told Dave anyway. To be honest, the chances of anybody tagging him and getting curious enough to investigate are pretty remote. Just don't want to be the only dork aboard, is all.

"I was sorry to hear about your father," Dave says. "He was a good man and a good friend."

Hiram nods. "It was his time. He's with mother now -- they'll both be with us always." He rubs his stomach and I want to retch. I hate dealing with ritual cannibals, but that's where the money is these days.

If Dave finds this as disturbing as I do, he doesn't give any indica-tion. "Otherwise, the husbands and wives doing well, I hope?"

Neo-pagans aren't just a cult, they're one big family, everybody married to everybody else.

"Some better than others, you know how it is," Hiram says, shrug-ging. "You are fine?"

"Enough of the small talk -- we're being charged for the call by the half-second." I take a laserstat of the storm out my sweater pocket, hold it up to the camera. "Recognize this?"

First he seems offended but then his eyes go wide and the glasses fall from his nose as he concentrates on the 'stat. "Uimon Rahn," he says with hushed reverence. "Mother-entity of the seventeen hungry demonics of Venerett."

"And a really nice person when you get to know her," I say, much less hushed and in no way reverent. "Which I have. Which you can. We can take you to her."

He looks at Dave. "What is this heretic talking about?"

"Forgive him for being a heretic, but it's his way. He is serious, though. He took that picture in orbit around Jupiter."

Hiram leans forward and for a moment I think his hair is gonna topple him over before he gets his balance. "A Holy Apparition... a vision... there are prophecies of such, but honestly, I always thought they were stories. Harmless ice-breakers before the orgies, that's all."

Known about the bogus neo-pagan prophecies all along, naturally. Gave me the idea in the first place, and reason I figured I could exploit this so easily. Religion tends to turn off those circuits in the brain that normally make somebody question spending vast sums of money. In this case, the vast sums I'll ask for could buy the neo-pagans three ships of their own, but these are neo-pagans who eat their own dead. Can they be all that smart?

"Don't know about any prophecies," I say, tucking the picture away. Hiram's eyes follow it greedily until it's in my pocket. "But I do know if you want to go see the Holy Apparition for yourself, we can help you. Telling you, the picture doesn't do it justice."

Hiram sits back. His face is resolute, no hint of hesitation. "Name your price."

Do I know my religious fanatics or what?

"Hope I'm not interrupting anything," I say, pushing off from the doorframe and flying at the far wall. Pluck a cannette of "God's Own Vengeance" beer from the netting ball floating in the center of the small cargo bay as I drift past.

"Well, matter a fact..." Dave says from somewhere above me. Can't see his expression but the tone in his voice says he's not at all happy to see me. Not that he ever is lately, but tonight, he's even more so.

Dave and the neo-pagans are strapped onto the walls, ceiling and floor, in clusters. Lights are low, there's the smell of patchouli, sweat, weed, and chocolate in the air. Nobody's completely naked yet, so I'm not too late for the orgy, thank god.

"Good. Hate to go someplace I'm not wanted." Squeeze in-between two of the women. They're a bonded pair, a silver chain strung between their ankles connecting them and signifying their special union within the cult's general union. They usually never play with others, and never outside the cult, on pain of losing the leg the chain is attached to, but it is gonna be a long trip and I'm an optimist. "--How you ladies doin'?"

Unveiled distaste in their expressions, they wince and look away even as I revel in the warmth of being pressed between them. I smile up at Dave, bowing his head, embarrassed. Love making him do that. "Everybody knows Jim, right?" he asks.

I pop the tab on the beer and squirt half of it down my throat. Course they all know me, all the women at least. We've been underway for three days now and I've done what any self-respecting tour guide should: Made it a priority to personally greet every last one of the two-dozen women aboard, let them know I'm at their disposal and that everything on me still works as god -- any god, take your pick -- intended. Even cornered the marginally ugly ones. Hundred-and-two, can't be all that picky.

No nibbles yet, but we've got fifteen more days of travel for them to come around.

Any luck, tonight's bacchanalia will get one or more of them in the mood to try a more seasoned specimen of manhood than their regular Renaissance-coiffed and powdered neo-pagan diet.

"So," I say, trying to resurrect the conversation my entrance brought to an untimely death, "what's everybody got going tonight? When's the sex start? I'm not getting any younger and I like to be in bed by nine."

They either stare at me like I'm some kind of incomprehensible alien, or whisper jokes or comments amongst themselves -- loud enough for me to hear some of the ruder ones, but I've developed quite a thick skin over the years. All except Hiram. Ever the leader, the politician, he smiles at me wistfully. "Your business partner..."

"--Former business partner," Dave quickly points out. I think I've pissed him off, for shame. "This is a one-time association here."

Hiram nods. "Former business partner, yes. Dave was about to tell us how you discovered the Holy Vision."

"Was he?" I ask through tightened lips.

"Yes. But now that you are here, perhaps you could tell us yourself. Dave is a dear friend, and we all respect him immensely, but this story will become legend among my people, and it would be a crime if we did not hear it from the source. For the sake of accuracy. This does not offend you, friend Joseph?"

"Not at all. --Yes, why don't you tell the nice people what you were doing at Jupiter, Artie? I'm sure they'll find it as hysterical as I did... I still wake up nights laughing about it."

He thinks he's tweaking me, forcing me into revealing deep, dark secrets to total strangers, but he obviously hasn't gotten to the juicy part, the part he wants me to embarrass myself by telling. So, no reason to tell. Boring, anyway. I'll make a good story better by embellishing.

Hiram and the neo-pagan generations to come will appreciate it all the more.

"Well," I say, affecting my best Jimmy Stewart manner, "it's nothing to write home about, really. It all started when I hired Cap'n Bobby to help me track down some pirates that were using Europa as an ops base for staging ore raids into the Belt, causing some trouble for some friends of mine. You've probably heard of them -- the United Belt Confederacy. I do some troubleshooting for them, every now and again."

Out of the corner of my eye, I see Dave slowly wince. But everyone else is captivated. It's the rare person who doesn't enjoy a good pirate tale. Even the two bonded chicks I'm nuzzled between are looking at me a little more warmly.

There may be sex in this for me yet tonight. I'll have to thank Dave later for the opportunity.

***

"Jim, I'm having second thoughts."

Eleven days into the journey and Dave has officially gone completely senile. Honestly, I'm surprised it took him that long.

I sit up in the cot. Ship's under deceleration for Jupiter orbital insertion. Will take us five days to slow which means we've got gravity until then. Been sleeping like a baby, my body never comfortable in zero-gee, a blood-flow thing. Also been sleeping alone, none of the pagan chicks yet won over by my charms. But I'm still optimistic. I've made serious progress in the last week -- they don't necessarily turn tail when they see me coming down a corridor, and once or twice I've caught my ass being admired. It is a round-trip, after all.

So, I'm in a good mood. Good enough to put up with Dave's senility and being woken from sleep. I smirk gently at him. "Shit -- when did I miss the first thought?"

He's sitting on the edge of his cot across. "Fuck you. No, listen, I think we ought to give Hiram back half his money. We're charging way too much for this."

I roll my eyes and give my head a little, exasperated shake. "Fine. Give him back your half. I'll keep mine. Everybody's happy."

"Thought we could do it even, both bite the bullet."

"The only bullet I'll be biting is the honking huge gold one I buy with the proceeds from this little pilgrimage."

"That's not exactly fair."

"That's not exactly my problem."

"You know, I'd thought maybe you'd changed. You're still a bastard. Taking advantage of their beliefs like this..."

"I'm a bastard?" I chuckle. "Look, I know what this is about. The neo-pagans are starting to accept me. Maybe even like me. That's pissing you off. I'm getting into 'Dave' territory and you want to be the most-favored-nation again by giving back their money."

"Like you? They can barely tolerate you."

"You just keep telling yourself that, Mister People-Person, if it helps your digestion. By the way, how is your digestion, lately, there, Davey? Still missing the old warm-and-fuzzy mind-altering drug feeling you used to be able to wallow in before your body started rebelling, no doubt from having to put up with your self-righteous, self-centered, holier-than-thou attitude all these years? I know I'm getting fed up and I've only had to deal with it for two weeks. If it wouldn't kill you instantly I'd force-feed you a handful of happy-pills myself just to get some fuckin' peace and quiet. No, wait, I'm to the point I don't care whether it would kill you or not."

His leather-old face shows the sting, his wrinkles quivering. For a second I think he's gonna go all hormonal and cry. "I should never have come. You haven't changed."

"Got that right. On both counts." I lay down. Turn onto my side, back to him. "Now, unless you're going to go get one of the pagan women and bring her back here by way of apologizing for interrupting my sleep, I suggest you go away before I decide I'm in a violent mood."

"It's not here anymore, is it?" Dave asks, breaking the long silence and tossing the cannette of beer he's been nursing down the corridor.

I shake my head. "Must have dissipated while we were in transit."

The three of us have been huddled around the big dorsal obs port for the better part of a quarter-hour, since Bobby put us in geo-synch roughly above where the storm-face of Uimon Rahn should be. Say should be because it has become obvious that the face is no longer there. The storm is there, but its shape has drastically changed, become more oval, flattened out, and it looks like parts of it have swirled off into a second storm trailing behind it.

Cap'n Bobby chews on his lower lip, skewing his chemically-induced translucent, Belter-tattooed face into an even more than usual unflattering piece of abstract art. "Those southern hemi storms are pretty volatile. Come and go, reform and reshape, all the time."

"You couldn't have told us this before now?" Dave asks him, none too kindly.

"He told me," I say, stepping in to defend the Cap'n. "Thought we could beat the odds, move fast enough."

Dave snaps around to glare at me. "You knew there was a chance it'd be gone? And you still dragged me out here?"

"There wasn't a gun to your head."

"Wish there was one to yours."

He's still upset, been that way since I threatened to kill him. God, he's gotten sensitive and unforgiving after hitting one-hundred. The old Dave would have pulled a knife on me soon as I turned my back to him and we would have settled things the old fashioned way, with blood spilled and a round of beers afterwards. Instead, he just left and brooded. I miss the old Dave -- he was a hell of a lot more fun at parties.

"So, what do we do?" Cap'n Bobby asks, looking nervously back and forth between me and Dave.

Dave snorts. "Give their money back, apologize profusely, and hope they understand these things happen."

"Are you insane? No refunds," I say. "Ever. Says so right in the contract."

"They don't strike me as understanding types," Cap'n Bobby says. "There'll be trouble if you can't keep your promise, won't there?"

Dave answers for me. "If they only eat Jim, we'll be lucky."

Bobby runs a ham-fingered hand through his tangled, crusty hair. "Fucking great. So what do we do?"

"Well, we don't tell them, for starters," I say.

Cap'n Bobby grits his teeth. "No shit. I say we leave orbit. Head for the Belt."

"That's as good as telling them the vision viewing's off," Dave says. He take a fresh beer cannette from a pouch on his belt and opens it. Smiles at it. The bastard's enjoying this. "We'll never make it."

I smirk at him. "We're not leaving. Not yet. First, we stall."

Dave is skeptical. "Stall?"

"Yeah, what else?" I ask, rhetorically. "Shutter the ship, don't let them see out by window or camera. Tell them there's a Wanaker-class radiation storm out there whipped up by an exceptionally active magnetosphere disturbance due to a polar shift."

"That's complete technobabble bullshit, you know that, don't you?" Cap'n Bobby protests.

"Sure, but if you say it, they'll believe it. People always believe the Captain. Genetic, I think."

"I don't like it, but what choice do I have?" The Cap'n twists a rusting dial at the edge of the portal and thick plates slide down over it, obscuring the view. "What're we stalling for?"

"A miracle. That the storm reforms into something approximating a neo-pagan god."

"And when that doesn't happen?" Cap'n Bobby asks.

I shrug. "Then I guess you get to see how to properly prepare a nine course Jim-themed meal."

"Well," Dave says, pausing dramatically to sip his beer, "at least there's that silver lining."

Stalling is a sucker's plan, I admit, but it's the only plan I got. I just don't think as fast as I did even a decade ago. And the hole in my head that was -- until the surgeons yanked it out -- my connection to the uberworld of the galactic computer network and its vast databases of knowledge is another, more tragic, handicap. A month ago I could have called up a database and consulted experts all from the comfort of my head over a distance-irrelevant etheralnet modem, figured out exactly how to get us out of this jam, and done it with panache. But that's not an option anymore. I could call up the same networks using the ship's computers, but Cap'n Bobby is cheap and has low-bandwidth equipment, good for voice and video only, not the high-speed uberworld streams. It would be like swimming upstream in peanut butter, and in flat two-d at that, my immersive systems also gone thanks to misuse, age and a couple botched home-surgery repair attempts. What's the point?

So, I let Dave and Cap'n Bobby do the thinking. Probably a suicidal move, that, but not exactly the first one of those I've made recently, is it? They huddle together for hour on end, working up elaborate plans, only to abandon them when they remember that they are stuck on a ship filled with dozens of intense, spiritually fervorish cannibals and there's only the three of us.

Me, I lounge, drink as many beer cannettes as possible, and wait for the inevitable.

The neo-pagans aren't stupid -- okay, not that stupid. They know we've been in orbit for two days. They know the planet's atmosphere does a full rotation every ten hours. They can do basic math, I presume. They have to be wondering why we're really keeping the ports closed, why we haven't shown them any external views. It's what they came here for, and after all the talk and build-up during the trip, here we are keeping the great holy vision under wraps. Don't think they believe the radiation storm story. There are grumblings amongst their ranks, accusing glances when they pass me in the corridors. The girls have stopped smiling at me completely, and I've been on my best behavior.

Probably too late refund their money.

"They've got the front end of the ship: the cargo bays, living quarters, machine shop, engines, and the big one, the bridge. Some good news, while I was running for my life, I managed to lock down the two corridors between here and there, which leaves us this mess hall, the emergency exit hatch, and a supply closet of toilette paper and cleaning supplies." Cap'n Bobby finishes his report between hard breaths. "So, they have everything but food and control of the ship."

Dave raises the left half of his unibrow. "But you said they have the bridge..."

"First thing I did when they boarded was slap a couple extra layers of security over the control systems. The ship'll only listen to me, and only after an authorization routine."

"Nice one," I say.

"Thanks, but it won't last long. I assume they know how to break security systems?"

"They're some of the best hackers out there. It's how they pay their bills. That and their restaurant chain."

"Then we're screwed, sooner or later," Bobby says, disheartened.

"We've still got computer access, though, right?"

"Yeah."

I feel a spark of encouragement. "Then you can order the ship to head for the belt, or cut off life support to their part of the ship. No point being cautious now that the cat's out of the can."

Cap'n Bobby shakes his head. "Part of the security system is a DNA sample for commands that critical."

I close my eyes and pinch the bridge of my nose. "And the sampler's on the bridge, right?"

"You got it. Only one aboard," the Cap'n says, frowning.

The intercom crackles with loud static, stops me from saying something insulting about his lack of planning.

"Attention heretics, betrayers, and our former friends," Hiram says over the ship-wide, equal parts of disgust and glee in his voice. Sounds like he's been drinking. "As soon as possible, we will attempt to appease the many gods and goddesses your actions have offended by performing a ritual Apology for the Damned. Since the ritual calls for a glorious Fire of Dignity, as the centerpiece of the ceremony, we will direct this ship to plummet into Jupiter's atmosphere. Despite our feelings towards you, we will allow you to share in the Holy Sacrifice we have decided to undertake in hopes that your next lives will share in the coin of our beneficence. Have a nice day."

The intercom goes quiet.

"Oh, just fuckin' great," I say, putting my head in my hands, rubbing my temples with my index fingers.

Dave asks the Cap'n, "Can they do that?"

"Even if they don't break the security systems, they have the engines. They could physically damage them easily enough. Ain't hard to imagine a couple ways they can deteriorate our orbit with a wrench whack."

I bite my lower lip. "What kind of semi-AI computer the ship running?"

"What's that matter?"

"If I know, I can estimate how long it will take them to break in. If it's longer than two days, we can then assume they'll just blow us up -- they'll get hungry by then. It'd give us a time frame, at least."

"Well, shit, you can do better than that, Artie. You can just hack into the ship's computer before they do." He turns to beam at the Cap'n. "The pagans are good, but Jim's better," Dave says.

"Why, that's an excellent idea, friend Dave," I say, letting my voice fill with irony and vitriol. "Why didn't I think of that? It is, after all, something I am more than capable of, having spent my life slipping in and out of computer systems with my trusty neural interfaces and bio-melded control circuitry and taking advantage of my natural-born ability to talk computers into anything I want simply by speaking to them on their own level. Why, I'll just dial up the ship's computer right now..."

I lift my left palm close to my face, wait a beat then make my eyes go wide dramatically and turn my scarred palm out to face him. "Oh, my, what's this? All my trusty equipment is gone? Oh, dear. How did that happen?" I sneer. "They took it all out or me, remember? Fucking insensitive moron."

"I forgot, okay? Sorry."

"Forgot, my ass. Muddle-headed senile coot."

"Wrinkled sex-mad asshole."

The Cap'n breaks in. "Snapping at each other won't help."

"No, no it won't," I say, "but it'll pass the time until the pagans come to collect us for brunch."

"They wouldn't," Bobby says, voice cracking with fear.

Dave nods dourly. "They will."

"Their religion, such as it is, requires it," I confirm. "They'll wait a bit, probably until right before we start to hit atmosphere, then they'll have themselves a feast. Eat us while the ship burns up as part of the sacrifice."

"I don't want to be eaten. And I don't want to lose my ship." Cap'n Bobby turns to me, his tattooed face right in mine. Got breath like a barn cat. "This is all your fault. You got me into it, you get me out of it. Okay, asshole?"

"You didn't have to take the charter," Dave hisses, ever present smile vanishing into a steely-eyed scowl. He puts one shaking hand on Bobby's shoulder while the other pulls a five-inch barbed ice-pick from his boot and holds its point unsteadily a centimeter in front of Bobby's left eye. "And I hear you call Artie that again, I'm gonna offer your eyeball to Hiram as an hors d'oeuvre. Understand?"

The backpedaling begins. "I'm sorry...didn't mean anything...but you just called him..."

"That's different. We've known each other for ninety plus years. You, I've just met and I'm damned sure you haven't earned it, yet. Now, do you have anything constructive to say, Cap'n?"

His face goes blank and he takes a moment to catch his breath. "What are we gonna do?"

Dave's smile returns and he lets go of the Cap'n, slipping the ice-pick away. He looks at me and I immediately know what he's thinking. It's almost like old times. Very old times. How depressing is that?

"Well, only one thing for it," he says. "Hoped it wouldn't come to this, but..."

"Yeah," I say, sighing. "Doesn't look like we got a choice. Time to call in our undead attorney."

Bobby arches an eyebrow. "I don't know what I should be more disturbed about -- the 'undead' or the 'attorney' part of that."

I purse my lips. "The attorney bit."

"Oh, shit yeah, definitely," Dave says.

Chris is as old as me and Dave but he doesn't look a day over twenty-five. That's because he died when he was twenty-five. Shot in the back seventy-four times with a rail-gun pistol by a disgruntled client. Why he doesn't do divorces anymore. Not worth the trouble.

Nano-resurrectionists did a pretty damn good job, though, and he's had additional work done since. Got a nose job, for starters, and had his forehead raised three inches to give him a brainier, more sophisticated look.

Took him sixteen hours to get to us from the Belt. Would have taken anyone else three times as long. Benefit of being dead -- seven-gee acceleration is a walk in the park.

"Jim, Dave," he says with that voice the undead have, raspy and breathless. Literally. He pulls himself through the docking ring and extends a perfectly normal-looking, room-temperature hand. "You must be in some kind of trouble to call me."

I sum it up for him. "Neo-pagans control the ship. Sometime in the next seven hours they're gonna break through the security systems and surf us into Jupiter."

"That all?"

"What, you want giant mutant rats out to take over the world, too?"

"Guess not. How'd this happen?"

Dave's turn. "Jim scammed them."

"But of course. Okay -- so am I here to evacuate you or negotiate a peace? I brought the small and fast ship, but it's got sleeper coffins that'll get you to the Belt without much permanent harm, I keep the gees low."

The Cap'n looks at me hard and pleading. We'd been over this again and again while we waited for Chris to arrive and decided to abandon ship and have Chris take us back to the Belt, nothing the neo-pagans can do to stop us. Well, me and Dave decided. Cap'n Bobby wants to save his ship, the selfish bastard.

I give Bobby a shrug sorry and turn to answer Chris.

"Peace," Dave says before I can say anything. "If you can. And Bobby control of his ship back."

I almost haul off and slap him but his body's so old his bones would probably shatter if I just touched him, and I can't be bothered to screw around with a skin bag of jellied Dave right now. So I glower at him instead. Isn't as satisfying but he does have that ice-pick, let's remember. "That's not the plan..."

He smiles back at me, smug. "It is now."

He's been planning this all along, I can tell. Thinks we owe something to Bobby for getting him into this. Fuck that.

Chris has known us long enough to know when to stay out of things. "Okay, which way am I headed?" he asks, keeping efficiently to business.

"Down here," Dave says, guiding Chris down the corridor towards the locked-down hatch to the neo-pagan section of the trawler. "They'll agree to talk to you, let you in, if we ask nice and they think they'll be able to eat you."

Chris puts his game face on, an unreadable mask of professional dead piranha. "Joke's on them, right?"

"He's an actual attorney?" Cap'n Bobby asks.

"Yeah, of course," Dave says. "What'd you think he was?"

"I thought it was some kind of euphemism. Like for mad-dog killer commando or something."

I snort. "Wouldn't that have been nice?"

We're in the mess hall again, our home for the past day, worried and wondering what the hell is taking Chris so long -- it's been three hours so far.

I have been uncharacteristically silent since Dave betrayed me. Tethered myself into a corner and floated there sulking, refusing to speak or be spoken to, listening with the bemused detachment of extreme old age to my body creak and groan, my heart barely managing to pump enough blood to keep my fingers and toes from tingling with numbness. Damn micro-grav.

We should be heading for the Belt right now, safe and sound in Chris' ship, tucked into comfortable if cramped living-dead life-support coffins. Instead we're trying to negotiate with flesh-eating religious fanatics and probably blowing any chance we have of getting out of this alive.

So, looks like I'll be taking that suicide run after all. For some reason, that thought brightens my mood immeasurably.

"What's your fucking problem?"

Look and Dave has floated up to me.

"What?" I ask.

"Your problem. This whole suicide kick of yours."

"Where did this come from?"

"I've been thinking. It's almost as if you counted on the neo-pagans doing something like this. Or at least hoped for it."

I don't look at him. I pick a spot on the wall below me, a microwave oven that needs a good cleaning. "Why would I do that?"

"Because you couldn't off yourself. No guts to go through with it, so you purposely try to piss Hiram off to do it for you."

"That's insane. The reason I didn't go through with it is I saw an opportunity, that's all. Never waste an opportunity, even if you have to change your plans."

"No, I think Dave's got a point, there," Cap'n Bobby says, from across the mess.

"Shut up," Dave and I both say, almost simultaneously. He does.

Dave's voice drops to a whisper. "You never told me why you went to Jupiter in the first place. Why you wanted to suicide. It's your implants, right? That's gotta be it. They got yanked out and now you don't see any point to living anymore. You always valued those machines more than anything else. More than your friends, more than yourself."

Idiot. Here I was thinking he had a clue. "Yeah, that's it. You guessed it right there, pal. Should've never figured on getting that past you."

He has no trouble detecting the sarcasm. "Fine, then, be that way. You want to stay all emotionally knotted up and alone, I'm not gonna stop you -- I give up. You know, I thought my not going to Hiram and talking him out of this -- which I could have done, by the way, 'cause he likes me, at least he did before this -- would bring you out of this fuckin' funk you've been in, give you a chance to do something spectacular like the old days, even without your implants. But looks like I was wrong. You just don't care anymore, do you?"

"Now that you mention it, no, no I don't."

He looks at me like I'm the insane one. "Why the fuck not?"

I take a deep breath, another. "We led armies, Davey. Brought down governments and corporations who trembled at the very thought of us knocking at their door. We were important. We did things. But we were young. When was the last time we were relevant? Twenty years, man, that's the last time anybody hired us for our skills -- because we were the only ones that could get the job done -- and not out of nostalgia. I'm tired of running tiny, unworthy scams in the Belt, cheating children and old women for pocket change. I've become a pathetic old man."

"So, who hasn't? It's called getting old. Slack off, take it easy. Enjoy yourself."

"Enjoy myself? How? You may think interning yourself in a dead-end-nothing-but-a-place-to-die-hell-hole like Gerald Ford is a viable option, but I don't. I've got a little more respect for myself than that."

"Respect?" He laughs, but it's a soft laugh. "Yeah, right. I think you're just scared."

I shrug defensively. "Scared of what?

"Of admitting you need to be looked after, would enjoy being looked after. There's no shame in that, man. It's the nature of things."

My turn to laugh and there's nothing soft about it. It's practically hysterical. "Wrong, oh so wrong. I'll tell you what I'm scared of, Davey-o. Having to put up with you every day and not having a bottle of cyanide to wash my troubles away with."

He doesn't say anything. Doesn't have the chance. The sound of the locked-down hatch in the corridor opening gets our attention.

Is this it, are neo-pagans going to be rushing us? Is it time for lunch, time to finish what I started three weeks ago before getting distracted by the idea of one last score?

"Okay, here's the sit," Chris announces as he pulls himself through the mess hatch, broad smile of victory on his obscenely high fore-headed face. My mood both plunges and elevates. He's emerged from negotiations unscathed, may have found us a way out, and I don't know whether to feel good or bad about that.

He floats up to us, Cap'n Bobby following him. "You three have been very, very naughty. Manipulating strongly-held religious beliefs to con a trusting group of true-believers into parting with large sums of money for the promise of a sacred experience that never materialized. Can't you just hear the pathos dripping off that?"

I sigh. Should have expected something like this. "Who's side are you on?"

"They've got a good case. Honestly, if this went before a jury, even considering they're cannibals, not the type to generally sway juror sympathies, the outcome would be almost certainly in their favor. Especially with me arguing their side. I'm very good with juries."

"You undead bastard. We brought you here to help us."

"And I have. The neo-pagans aren't going to blow up the ship, or perform any suicide rituals."

"When do I get my ship back?" Cap'n Bobby asks, excited and relieved.

"That's why we call it negotiations, son," Chris says. "You don't. It's theirs, now. They've already broken the security measures, so no need to trouble yourself lifting them, but you will have to officially turn over title, all that. They've agreed to give you an hour to do so. Plenty of time."

Cap'n Bobby's voice rises into a harsh whine. "Bullshit. No way I'm..."

"Tough break, Bobby," I say, interrupting him. "It's for the best, though. Probably."

He glares at me. "For the best? You fuckin' lost me my ship."

For a moment I think he's gonna charge at me, but a look from Dave, cleaning his teeth with the ice-pick, persuade Cap'n Bobby to keep calm.

"He did, indeed," Chris agrees, guiltlessly. "They will be needing a pilot, though. Hiram's promised to work out a competitive wage and benefits package, captain. I can negotiate on your behalf, for an industry-standard agent fee."

Cap'n Bobby is stunned silent. In his eyes I see he's seeing his life crumble before him, all thanks to me. Glad I could be of service.

Chris takes his silence as acceptance. "Fine, I'll get to work on that as soon as we take care of handing over the ship. Now, as for your two," he says, pointing a lifeless finger at me and Dave, "you understand my clients would prefer you not dirty their new ship with your presence?"

"Wait, let me guess, they want us to jump out the nearest airlock?"

"Not at all, although if you're volunteering... No? Then, they've agreed to let me give you safe passage back to the Belt. From there, you're on your own. Go wherever you want, with the promise of no reprisals, unless you come within a planet's circumference of my clients again. At which point, you will be tracked down and eaten." Chris purses his pale lips. "So, where to, gentlemen?"

Time for both Dave and I to go silent. Dave looks at me, and I know what he's thinking. I allow myself a second or two to savor the still-fresh thought of plunging into Jupiter, close my eyes and imagine how sweet that would feel. Certainly feel better than being an impotent old man who can't even get himself out of his own scrapes anymore, has to call in hired undead help.

I open my eyes and I can't bring myself to look Dave in the face again, for fear he'll gloat. I lock eyes with Chris.

"Place called Ford Long Term, at L5," I say, my mouth dry. "Hear the robots let you play with their insides, if you behave. And I always behave."

Dave breaks into a stupid grin. Moron. Wait until I whip his ass for the hundredth-thousandth time at chess, see how much he smiles then.

Nine

HELMET TIME

CHARLES AOKI WAS GETTING the crap beaten out of him again.

Manert could call it a friendly boxing match if he wanted, but that didn't change the fact that it was really nothing more than a convenient way for the robot to keep his combat skills honed and Aoki ever-mindful he was a slave.

The battlesuit Manert let Aoki wear–to make it more of an even fight, so the robot claimed–didn't so much help as hinder, truth be told. Sure it enclosed Aoki in what was for all intents and purposes a miniature tank, surrounding him in several layers of good old-fashioned armor plating and mechanically enhancing his strength through hydraulic and composite muscles, but it had been built for a zagonty. A large zagonty, to boot–twice Aoki's size and with an extra pair of arms. Aoki felt like a three-year old wearing his father's cowboy boots. He was only loosely strapped in. Every time Manert struck him, Aoki's body would bounce around inside the suit, causing more collateral damage than direct.

Aoki couldn't control the suit very well, either. It had neural interfaces, but again, for a zagonty's nervous system. Aoki's puny little human nervous system couldn't even get the attention of the on-board computers. He had to run the suit with a combination of verbal commands—in zagonty, of course, which he spoke only haltingly and with an accent the computer had trouble deciphering—and manual dexterity, his normal lack of which made all the more awkward by Manert's insistence that gravity in the gym be set at a hearty 2.3 of Earth gee.

Manert was in one of his smaller combat bodies this session. The robot looked like some kind of twenty-legged insect, all shiny black composite alloy legs and limbs. Each limb was tipped with a different kind of weapon. Blades, spiked balls, hooks. The legs had giant, clawed tripods for feet. Manert liked to kick with those. From the right angle, they could even dent the armor of Aoki's battlesuit.

When Manert moved, it was an unstoppable swirl of death. Faced with that, all Aoki wanted to do was roll into a ball on the floor and let the suit absorb as much as it could. But Manert didn't like it when Aoki went passive. If Aoki tried to go into a fetal position on the floor, Manert would send a remote-control pulse to the battlesuit and force it into the standard hand-to-hand fighting position, feet set apart, knees slightly bent, lower arms back preparing to strike, upper arms raised in a semi-relaxed defensive position. Then Manert would launch an even more vigorous attack than usual, upset that Aoki wasn't "giving it his all."

So Aoki would play along, get up every time he was knocked down, and get into the stance on his own. Sometimes he'd try to throw a punch or something equally futile, but inevitably he would end up on the floor again after another few seconds that seemed like hours of Manert wailing at him.

He consoled himself that it would be over soon. Usually the sessions lasted more than an hour, but this time, Manert only wanted to get in a quick ten minutes before they arrived in the Rithec system.

Aoki kept stealing glances at the big clock on the gymnasium wall. Nine minutes had gone by, albeit excruciatingly slowly, already.

Aoki was pulling himself off the floor and into the defensive stance yet again when the gymnasium lights flicked. He didn't look after the cause until he saw that Manert was already doing so himself.

Skeen stood at the arched entrance to the gym, looking like some badly sculpted laughing Buddha, her thick, segmented tail swishing absently. One hand was on the light panel, another wrapped around a mug filled with something noxious. Red steam rose from the mug. "If I can interrupt, boys? We're in Rithec. It looks like there's a real fight going on."

"Good. This has put me in the mood most satisfactorily." Manert disengaged his central cylindrical core—the physical repository of his main personality—from the combat rig and skittered along the floor on spindly legs to attach himself to his work-a-day general purpose body. "Chuck," he said to Aoki, "as always, you were a challenge."

Aoki didn't believe that for a second. It was just something Manert always said, and just like always, Aoki said back, "Thank you, sir." He wasn't thanking Manert for the false compliment, he was thanking him for the fight being over.

"Get yourself cleaned up and stow my battle body, then join us on the bridge."

"Sure."

Aoki watched the robot and the mitnic leave the gym, then started peeling himself out of the battlesuit. He took it as easy and slow as he could, favoring his left arm, which he figured was fractured, if not broken. He hoped he'd be able to sneak into the auto-doc to have it looked at some time in the near future. By the weekend, at least.

There wasn't much for Aoki to do on the bridge. Most of the important systems in the battleship–those that neither Manert nor Skeen trusted him to run–were either automated or run by one of them. The offense and defense systems fell into that category. Manert ran most of those by plugging himself into an interface console in the ceiling of the bridge. Skeen played her part by taking the Captain's chair, directing the automated supplemental systems like engineering and life support by way of a bulky hundred-button remote control.

This left Aoki a spectator at times like these. He didn't mind that at all. It was one of the few times he was expected just to sit back and keep out of the way, not do anything but watch. It was the closet he ever got to a vacation.

Aoki was expected to watch through an immersion helmet, connected to the ships systems, which presented him with the solid illusion he was the ship itself. He sighed, took the helmet from its hook on the side of his stool, and slipped it over his head.

The *Prideful Punishment* was over eight-hundred years old. Built by the zagonty back when the order of the day was still intimidation by size, the *Punishment* was a three-hundred meter long, four-hundred meter high, half-billion ton death machine designed specifically to enforce the peace using a combination of massive ordinance and fear. When the zagonty had given the ship to Manert in recognition for his two-hundred years of service as a retirement gift, they'd stripped it of most of the really devastating weaponry, but its sheer size and the number of smaller weapons it carried still made it more than a match for anything outside the various Domesticate militaries. Nothing else in the civilian sphere of things could challenge it.

It was that fact that had led Manert into his post-retirement career of self-appointed protector of the fringes. The robot saw himself as a noble vigilante, guarding the farthest reaches of the Corporatti from threats both internal and external, and in some small way, helping promote law and order by blowing up trouble-makers. The Corporatti knew of his activities, and although they, for reasons of public relations, had never officially endorsed his activities, they supported him unofficially, offering him deep, un-precedented discounts on ordinance and feeding him information through back-channels about trouble spots on the fringes they couldn't bother to spare their own resources to handle.

The helmet settled over Aoki's head, it clicked and hummed, then a new universe appeared in his consciousness. He always became unsettled when he was looking at the universe through the senses of the ship. He could see all of space around the battleship, without turning his head. He didn't have a head to turn, in any case. His eyes were a hundred cameras and sensors scattered over the skin of the *Punishment*. He was a limbless observer, with no ability to do anything. It gave him an odd feeling of detached, impotent omniscience.

He was plowing towards a planet on fire. The whole planet wasn't aflame, of course, and he couldn't actually see the hun-dreds of flaming outbreaks through the thick atmosphere, but he knew they were there. The infrared sensors told him that. From this distance the fires appeared small. Aoki realized at that scale, whole cities must have been burning.

Between him and the planet was a swarm of smaller ships. Dozens, their sizes ranging from a tiny skiff to a medium-sized cargo trawler.

Most of the ships were darting around the trawler, which was dragging some kind of cargo on a tether behind it.

The cargo, Aoki decided, was what the fight was about. With all the firepower being thrown around, it looked like everyone was taking care not to fire in its direction.

The *Prideful Punishment* must have registered on the combatants scanners then, as a few of the ships broke off to intercept, their trajectories fuel-wasting near-straight lines.

Aoki knew what was coming. He didn't feel like watching this time. His hand–somewhere so far outside his current field of perception he simply had to assume he still had control of it–found the feed toggle on the immersion rig control and flicked it.

Yet another universe bloomed inside him, and abruptly, he wasn't the ship anymore. He was himself, or at least the "self" he had defined and built up inside this elaborate virtual world over the past three years, which somehow felt more real, and definitely more enjoyable, than his real life.

In real life, he'd been sold into slavery by his parents when he was twelve as part of a bankruptcy settlement. It was either sell their oldest or give up their credit cards, and the latter just hadn't been a realistic option, not with Christmas so close. Aoki had passed through at least a dozen hands (or their equivalent) in the thirteen years since, starting with a stint as a valet for a clutch of lous merchants, and ending up with Manert and Skeen. He'd been in their service for two and a half years, now, the longest time he'd spent in anyone's possession. The general attitude of disrespect and laziness Aoki projected seemed to only endear him further to Manert and Skeen, instead of encouraging them to sell him as it had with most of his former owners.

Wearing the immersion helmet, inside his special, favorite program, his life couldn't have been more different than the reality. He had a perky, lovely wife, a precocious kid, a modest suburban house with a conversation nook, complete with ottoman, and neighbors who were also his friends. His days he spent as the head writer for a 1950's comedy-variety television show. He and his fellow writers spent most of their time trading quips and insulting their immediate boss. The whole thing was in black and white, low-resolution, the limited artificial intelligences playing his wife, staff and the other characters prone to repeating themselves. Still, he preferred it to his real life, and every second he could steal to enter his black-and-white world he considered more precious than gold. Or his actual freedom, sometimes.

The scene that greeted him was a familiar one. He was at the office, pacing, just having gotten off the phone with his wife, who'd called in a panic about something or other. He was trying to think up an opening monologue while wondering whether he should tell his staff about the odd walnut-filled dream he'd had the night before.

He'd been through this particular scenario a hundred times. It was one of his favorites. He settled in to the storyline, let it play itself out, happy just to be anywhere but a slave aboard the *Prideful Punishment*.

A few hours later, back in the real world, Aoki was out in the void and apprehensively thrusting towards the battered cargo sphere. As he did, it occurred to him he was spending way too much time in ill-fitting mechanical-assist suits lately and way too little time being a comedy show writer. Annoying more than depressing.

The EVA suit he was stuffed into was built for a heetz, four-foot tall semi-intelligent pets used for ship-board rat-catching and the occasional hull repair detail. He'd spot-welded two suits together, cut in half and joined at the waist, with generous application of epoxy over the joint to keep an almost air-tight seal. It only leaked a little, if he didn't move around inside it much. Which turned out not to be a problem, since there wasn't much room to move in to begin with. Barely enough room in the suit for him to take a deep breath.

The sphere hung in space before him, right where the *Punishment* had liberated it in the battle Aoki was supposed to have watched. Around it was a broad field of wreckage: Twisted alloy, floating bodies, drifting pools of oil and fuel. The *Punishment* had made short work of destroying all the salvagers. Not one ship had been able to get away.

Soon Aoki was close enough that the sphere filled his entire field of vision. Sensor readings scrolling along the left side of his helmet visor told him it was one hundred and twelve meters in diameter, on average, but he didn't need dry statistics to tell him it was big. He had eyes.

"Well?" Skeen asked. A gray-and-white camera view of the *Prideful Punishment*'s bridge clicked on in front of Aoki's forehead. Skeen sat sprawled in the captain's chair, a hover-table stacked high with light snacks and assorted mitnic intoxicants floating next to her. Manert hung from the ceiling, still fully wired into the battleship.

"Well, what?" Aoki replied.

"Do you see any way in?"

"No," Aoki said, scanning the surface of the sphere. It looked like some kind of huge fuel tank, its broad gray surface for the most part an uninterrupted skin of ten-meter wide panels, with some superficial scratches and scars from the fight with the salvagers. Or maybe the damage was from whatever disaster had brought it into the hands of the salvagers in the first place. He couldn't spot anything that might be an access port. There were odd meter-wide bumps every so often along the circumference, and on those bumps were big blue circles with zagonty lettering inside. Aoki knew that to the zagonty, blue was the preferred color of warning.

Aoki stopped his forward thrust.

"What're you doing?" Skeen asked over the suit radio. "Get closer to one of things. I want to see what the warning says."

"Use a camera zoom–this is as close as I get until I know what they are."

"If I wanted to use a zoom I would have asked for a zoom. I said get closer."

"Why isn't one of the robots doing this?" Aoki asked, curtly.

In the tiny view of the bridge, Aoki saw Skeen bare her food-grinding cartilage. "Because if something goes wrong, we can't afford to buy another robot."

Aoki grunted and hit the thrust, drifting slowly closer to one of the bumps. He couldn't read the zagonty warnings, but he could read the radiation detection notices the EVA suit was scrolling in front of nose.

"Shit. Those things are putting out rads." Aoki again stopped his forward thrust. This time, threat or no threat, he wasn't getting any closer.

"Oh, only tiny amounts. Wimp." Skeen squinted at something off-camera, obviously studying the feed from the EVA suit's camera. "It's a general warning. Nothing specific. I can make out 'CAUTION' and 'RESTRICTED', and some legalese. Chucky, get a little closer, boy."

Before Aoki could protest, and much to his relief, Manert spoke up at last. "That's all right, Aoki. Stay put." The robot had direct access not only to the EVA suit's sensors, but to the battleship's more extensive and powerful sensors as well. "They're bombs. Atomics."

Skeen sat forward, knocking the snack hover-table off-kilter. It wobbled heroically to retain its equilibrium. "Who in their right mind would strap atomics to a fuel tank?"

"It's not a fuel tank," Manert said, untangling himself from the interface console he was plugged in to. He dropped to the floor to squat next to Skeen. "There's only one thing it could be. A superluminal tubeway constructor."

Skeen's mouth dilated. She looked at her partner dubiously. "You're crazy."

"No, no I'm not. I just have access to more facts than you do."

"Do go on."

"Fact one, no-one straps atomics to a fuel tank, or any kind of tank. And the configuration of the atomics on the sphere wouldn't make for a good weapon. Their function is solely to self-destruct the sphere."

"All right. But it's still a big leap calling it a constructor."

"Fact two, there are three superluminal tubeway heads in this system. One belonging to the tubeway we came in from, and two belonging to a short tube a few degrees of orbit behind that planet."

"A short tube?"

"In an orbital path. Strikes me as strange as well."

Aoki broke in. "Hey, I can't tell you how interesting this conversation is, but I'm floating out here and my air levels are getting slightly toxic."

"You've got thirteen minutes until you can't breathe. Plenty of time to check out one of the atomics," Skeen said.

"Bullshit. Send a robot out."

"It isn't a good idea to get near the atomics," Manert interjected. "Since they are obviously a self-destruct mechanism, and they undoubtedly malfunctioned, the device may be unstable. At least in this case, I believe we can afford to use a robot. To determine if the atomics are armed, and disarm them if necessary."

"Fine," Skeen said. "It's you're lucky day, Chucky. Come back on in."

"Not so fast," Manert said. "I've sensed a loose panel on the secondary starboard plasma ejectors. You might as well fix it while you're out there."

"But that'll take a half-hour. I'll die half-way through."

"Don't be so dramatic," Manert said. "You won't die. I've analyzed the toxic nature of the EVA suit air and there's only a two-percent chance you'll suffer permanent mental degradation. Assuming you can get the job done inside of twenty-nine minutes, that is. After that, the percentage increases to over fifty percent."

Aoki watched Skeen lean forward, grab a large handful of snacks from the floating hover-tray. "I'd hustle if I were you, Chucky."

Aoki suddenly wished the EVA suit had a built-in immersion rig, so he could point himself towards deep space, hit the thrust, and snap on his preferred universe. The idea of dying while escaping both physically and mentally appealed to him, but he knew in his heart that he'd be "rescued" just before his final breath. And he'd still be expected to fix that damn loose panel, no doubt after Manert and Skeen magnanimously gave him a few minutes to refresh his air supply and gather his thoughts after such an ordeal.

As soon as Aoki was back aboard and had extricated himself from the EVA suit, Skeen called him to the Officer's galley to prepare lunch. Skeen was already there, lounging at a table impatiently. Manert was there, too, wearing his R&D body, the one with wheels and hundreds of on-board scientific, technical, and historical reference libraries.

Aoki immediately went to the kitchenette, pulling a cryo canister out of the fridge. He set the canister on the counter and activated it, then went to collect a plate and a loaf of fungus as the canister hummed away. When it stopped humming the lid popped open. Aoki reached in, grabbed the flash-revived and still groggy rodent-thing quivering inside, and twisted its neck until it snapped. He placed it on the plate along with the fungus and brought it to Skeen. The mitnic set to it with gusto, gesturing for Aoki to wait by the table in case he wanted something else.

"Now that the robots have stabilized the atomics, I have developed a scenario." Manert opened a panel on his torso and extended a holo-projector. An image of a generic life-bearing planet appeared in front of him. "This planet here is just going about its business, winding around its orbit like it's done since it was only a gas and dust swirl, its inhabitants blissfully ignorant of the rest of the universe outside their atmosphere. Then one day there's something new in the sky."

The planet grew small in the projection and the scene shifted to the left, where a wireframe cylinder slowly spewed a red-black glowing column from its rear.

"The tubeway being laid," Skeen said.

"Correct. Perhaps it's visible to the naked eye while its being laid, while it cools, so to speak. Or maybe the natives of our ignorant little world could see the signature electromagnetic frequencies."

Skeen sighed. "Or maybe they couldn't see it at all. It doesn't matter. Stop theorizing and get to the point."

Manert made an annoyed clicking sound, then the holographic image shifted again. The planet and tube as seen from high above the galactic plane. A faint dotted line traced the orbital path of the planet. The line neatly intersected with the tubeway.

"Somebody made a mistake, I think," Manert said. "A miscalculation. The zagonty must have accidentally placed the tube in the way of the planet."

The time-scale of the image sped up. Weeks passed in seconds as the planet drew closer to the tube. The image zoomed in on the planet as it was slowly bisected by the tubeway, a thin, dark red wire slicing easily through the planet. In the wake of the tube's passage, the planet's surface rippled as it collapsed back together.

"It must have been... catastrophic. We've seen the results. Destroyed the planet, made it uninhabitable. Impressive, yes? The space inside a tubeway isn't normal anymore. It's re-sewn to allow faster-than-light travel. The part of the planet that traveled through the tubeway material would have been accelerated. It wouldn't have taken much extra speed–the parts that came out the other side were maybe travelling a few hundred feet per second faster, if that, but it would have done the trick."

"You really think it was a miscalculation that caused all this?"

"Mistakes happen. Can't think they meant to do it on purpose–'course, I have heard some pretty disturbing stories about the lengths the Corporatti will go to for power or revenge, or just to prove a point to the Domesticates. Wouldn't surprise me at all if this was the result of some kind of lesson."

"I can see zagonty infighting taking out a planet, but not with a tube-layer. They're just too valuable to waste that way."

"Which is why I'm more apt to believe the accident theory. The planet hitting the tubeway could have created a shock wave down the length of the tube–that's probably how the tube-layer bought it. If it was still laying tube when the collision occurred, the shock wave would have taken it out nice and clean."

"And quickly."

"Instantaneous, maybe. Explains why they didn't have time to manually blow the atomics on the constructor. I imagine the constructor was set to automatically blow if the tube-layer was destroyed, but something must have gone wrong."

"Our luck it did."

Manert shut down the projection. "You could look at it that way, I suppose. Now we have to decide what to do with it."

"That's easy. We sell it." Skeen's nostrils flapped. Aoki could tell she was already counting the money.

"Can't do that, partner," Manert said.

"And why not? We'll find a buyer. I have connections."

"It's not that simple." Manert pointed a telemetry stalk at Aoki. "You can go now, Chucky."

They rarely let Aoki listen to business plans. "Sure, great, just when it's getting interesting." Aoki wiped his hands on a dishcloth. "Been wanting to get some helmet time in."

"Go right ahead. As soon as you suit back up and attach some tether lines to the constructor."

Aoki sighed. "Yeah, of course. Can I at least get the robots to help?"

"It you think you must. Anything happens to one of them—it's coming out of your food ration. Understood?"

"Yeah, of course."

It took Aoki the better part of the afternoon to rig the sphere up into a tether harness, even working with a trio of drone robots. By the time he was back aboard, it was dinnertime, and Skeen had wanted something special, which meant extra time in the kitchen. Then there was cleaning detail–decks fourteen through twenty-two that evening–and it was laundry day, to boot, so Aoki had to collect Skeen's things and run them through the extensive, complex process needed to excise the oils and sweat the mitnic constantly produced in copious amounts. That brought Aoki to about two in the morning, ship's time, leaving him two hours to himself before he was expected to be on the bridge to run the daily systems check.

He should have caught some sleep instead of jumping under the helmet, but it had been a long day, and he could always take some uppers to see him through. Helmet time was more important and pleasurable than sleep, anyway.

The scenario was another familiar one. This one was something of his own devising, entered into the helmet through a complex series of question-and-answers with the immersion control program, a psychological personality test to determine his true likes and dislikes, and what he'd find exciting to do inside. It centered around the night he and his wife finally pushed their beds together.

They were just sliding the beds together, giggling, lustful, when the universe ended.

"Hey, how's it going?" Skeen stood over him, her long slit of a mouth pinched into an oval showing off multiple rows of food-grinding cartilage, a mitnic smile.

Aoki skittered back in the bed, sitting up against the wall. He took the immersion helmet off and set it gently on a shelf above his head. He gave himself a moment to readjust to the real world, then cautiously returned the smile. "Just fine. Did I forget something? What time is it?"

"No, no, you didn't forget anything."

A wave of fear and trepidation spread over Aoki, a grip of absolute terror. If he hadn't forgotten a chore, there was only one thing he could think of that would bring Skeen to his cabin in the middle of the night. "Dear God," Aoki said, his voice cracking, "it isn't that time of year again, is it?"

"Not for another few months, Chucky. I just want to talk."

The terror left Aoki, joyfully replaced by confusion. "Talk? About what?"

Skeen pushed his legs aside and settled her bulk onto the end of the cot. It creaked, but didn't outright collapse. "I think I'm having an ethical dilemma."

Aoki nodded, and swore to himself. In some ways, Skeen's "ethical dilemmas" were worse than her being in heat. At least when she was in heat, Aoki's duties, however distasteful, were over inside of a few minutes. With Skeen's "dilemmas," there was no telling how long she'd expect him to lend an ear.

Her penchant for talking things out and general soul-rending over any number of decisions stemmed from her previous career. Straight out of the nest she had joined a mitnic equivalent of a monastery to live a life of quiet contemplation, pacifism, and self-denial. She'd been plugging along on that course for two decades when it suddenly occurred to her she probably would have more fun killing and raping for a living, so she up and quit the monastery and joined one of the thousands of Mitnic Domesticate terror squads. That's how she'd met Manert, during a joint Zagonty-Mitnic operation ten years back.

But her decades as a monk still influenced her, made her think about things much more than she needed to, in Aoki's opinion. Made her question everything, in the smallest detail sometimes, much to the annoyance of both Aoki and Manert, since she thought best aloud. She'd often corner one of them to talk. And talk. And talk.

Aoki resigned himself to not getting back into the helmet anytime soon, and asked, "This have something to do with the constructor?"

"Yeah. Manert says we have to give it back to zagonty."

Aoki shrugged. "It is theirs."

"I know. But it's such a waste."

"Seems to me it'd be too hot to sell."

"That's what Manert said, that the zagonty would make it their business to track down and punish whoever bought the thing, and whoever sold it."

"I see," Aoki said. "Sounds like a valid argument. I wouldn't want the whole Corporatti after me. Well, now that that's settled, can I go back to sleep?"

"You weren't sleeping, Chuck," Skeen said, knowingly nodding at the helmet. "Thing'll rot your brain, you know, and you humans don't have much to spare."

"Enough to do your dirty work."

"But not enough to do it well. But I'm not here to talk about your work habits, am I? No." Skeen leaned back, her eyes focusing on nothing in particular in the shadows on the ceiling. "I don't think Manert really understands what that constructor represents, what it could mean."

Here it comes. The dilemma. Aoki braced himself and decided to prompt her, hoping against hope he might speed things along. "What could it mean?"

"The tubeway technology, only the zagonty have it. It's one of the things that's let them conquer the galaxy. And as long as it's a monopoly, they'll stay in charge."

"Okay," Aoki said, not sure where Skeen was heading. "All the more reason for the zagonty to want the constructor back. They'll probably give you a reward for returning it, if it's that precious."

"The money's not important, Chuck. Not this time."

"Then what's the problem?"

"What would happen if another race got hold of the constructor, figured out how to use it to make its own superluminal network?"

Aoki shrugged cautiously. "The Corporatti would have some competition for once."

"Right. Competition brings change, evolution. The Corporatti hasn't evolved in any significant ways in over a thousand years–it's let itself get soft, become a bloated, stale creature."

Aoki leaned forward, her voice lowering. "So if another race got the constructor tech, if they wanted, they might be able to turn it into a chance to overthrow the zagonty, to get out from under the Corporatti's control, if they were lucky."

"Don't be ridiculous. Constructor technology alone doesn't make an interstellar empire. The zagonty have a dozen technological secrets, not just constructors, and they've got the biggest fleet, a bureaucracy in place, the loyalty of billions and the respectful fear of trillions."

As quickly as the idea of somebody, anybody overthrowing the zagonty had filled Aoki with hope, the feeling left, replaced by his usual apathy towards his life. Deflated, back to being a slave, he sighed. "If it's hopeless, why bother giving anybody else the constructor?"

"Haven't you been listening? I don't want to overthrow the Corporatti. I love the Corporatti–before they Domesticated my people, the mitnic weren't more than barbarians. They made us what we are today, second only to the zagonty themselves. And they made me what I am. I owe them everything." Skeen beamed with pride, puffing up her rib cage with a deep inhale. "No, I want to make the Corporatti stronger. A little competition could do that."

Aoki nodded solemnly. "Of course you do. Loyal to the core, that's my owner, Skeen. Make the zagonty even stronger. Got to love that idea. Did you tell Manert any of this?"

"I tried to explain, but Manert doesn't understand. He's got absolute loyalty to the zagonty programmed into his kernel, bless him. He can't even conceive of the possibility that letting another race in on the constructor technology might actually be good for the Corporatti. He thinks it'd be pretty much treason. And maybe he's right."

"I can see his point."

"So can I. Hence my dilemma."

"Rough. What're you going to do?"

"Do? I'm going to do nothing. It's Manert's ship. I'm only a quarter partner. And there's that treason angle."

"Good decision. Glad I could help." Aoki gestured at the hatch. "Now, if there's nothing else..."

"Well," Skeen said, again smiling, "all this talk has made me hungry. Let's you and me hit the galley, all right? We can continue this conversation over food."

Aoki winced, then swung his legs off the side of the cot. "Oh, like you can't make your own midnight snack?"

"You know, you're funny, sometimes."

The *Prideful Punishment* was taking its time heading back to the superluminal tubeway that would take them out of the system. Part of that leisurely pace was due to their cargo, strung out behind the battleship on its tether. Manert was fairly certain that if the atomics hadn't gone off already, they weren't going to at all, but there might have been something the robots, or more likely, Aoki, had done when the tether was rigged to reactivate the things. At least that's what he told Aoki.

The three of them were on the bridge, Skeen seated in her oversized captain's chair, Manert plugged into the ceiling, Aoki sitting off in the corner. Manert insisted that since it was slow, they had plenty of time to run a diagnostic of the ship's sub-systems. Well, Aoki had plenty of time. Skeen and Manert just watched Aoki at the command console, and chatted. They chatted about anything except the plan to hand the constructor over. That issue was settled.

Manert noticed the fleet first. He turned on a flatscreen near Aoki's head. A dozen ships, ranging in size, but all sleek and needlelike, transitioned out of the terminus of the superluminal tubeway.

They wouldn't be fighting this fleet. It was zagonty, for one thing. And even the smallest of the ships, no more than a skiff, could destroy the *Prideful Punishment* without much effort at all.

"Now, this is a surprise," Skeen commented, glancing at the flatscreen.

"Not really," Manert said. "It's the Third Fleet. I imagine the Corporatti dispatched it the moment they lost contact with the constructor. Let's hope Jur Ith is still in charge."

"She owes us one, doesn't she?" Skeen asked.

"More than one, as I recall. With any luck, she'll agree to take the constructor off our hands. Didn't feel like towing it all the way back to the zagonty homeworld."

As Aoki watched the fleet on the flatscreen monitor, the forward half of the bridge wavered, then filled with a holographic image. The flat, oval face of an enthak floated there. The zagonty preferred enthak liaisons, and used them almost exclusively as communication staff, the same way they used jharwin androids as lawyers, diplomats, and cops.

"I contact you on behalf of Admiral Jur Ith Nonev, commander of the Corporatti Militate Third Fleet, from aboard the flagship *Mutual Wife*," the enthak said, although its thin lips didn't move. A sub-vocal translator unit was pasted to its neck. "Please confirm that you are the *Prideful Punishment* under the command of Captain Manert 88475-293."

"That's me," Manert said. "How can we be of service?"

"You are in a restricted system. Please explain your presence."

"We often patrol the outer systems. Our presence tends to discourage illegal activity."

"Your public spirit is noted. Do you always patrol towing scrap?" the enthak asked. The question seemed a bit odd to Aoki.

"No, not at all," Manert answered. "We found it back near the planet. A couple of salvagers were fighting over it. We stopped them."

"Salvagers? I would think in a system this size they'd have more to fight over than a hunk of scrap, interesting as it is. It is interesting, isn't it?"

Something in the way the enthak had phrased that question made Aoki panic.

"Excuse me, Manert," Aoki said, pressing a button on the console next to him that made the communication screen go opaque. The enthak on the other end would see an entertaining and educational cartoon about farming, Skeen's idea of on-hold material. "I don't think you should tell them you know what the sphere is."

Manert swiveled his sensor stalk around and down towards Aoki. "Why not?"

"Just a feeling, but notice how they've avoided mentioning what it is themselves? And they seem really interested in finding out what we think it is... almost like they're trying to trick us into admitting we know what it is."

"What would be the point of that?" Skeen asked.

"Think about it," Aoki said. "They strapped atomics to the thing, which tells me they'd self-destruct a ship full of zagonty to keep the technology secret. I doubt they'd hesitate to blow us apart if they thought we knew. We're not zagonty, after all."

"Then why not just blow us up regardless?" Skeen asked. "Why bother trying to wheedle the info out of us? You're being a little too paranoid, even for a human, Chuck."

"It must be the Admiral," Manert said. "We have a history. She's giving us a chance to live."

Aoki nodded. "By not admitting we know it's a constructor."

"Yeah. Remind me to send her a case of something mind-altering. And re-open the channel."

Aoki hit the button again. The flat face of the enthak filled the front of the bridge again. Aoki could see guards preening and technicians working in the background. They seemed to relax a bit once they realized communications had been restored.

"Sorry about that," Manert said to the enthak. "Our slave's hand slipped."

"No apologies needed, Captain Manert. Humans–I often wonder why the Corporatti bothered to domesticate them instead of simply appropriating their world. They have a terrible reputation."

"I know, believe me I know. Thinking about trading this one in on a lous. Sure, they spit a lot, but at least they don't grouse constantly. Now, before we were interrupted, you were saying?"

"The scrap you're towing. I was saying how interesting it is. Ever seen anything like it before?"

"Can't say I have. Fuel tank or something, I figured. Wonderful workmanship, I'll say that."

"Yes," the enthak said, his eye-sockets widening. "Wonderful workmanship."

"So, do you want it? I mean, do you have a claim to it? If you do, it's yours. Probably wouldn't fetch much as scrap, in all honesty."

"We can take it off your hands, yes. You will be paid for its recovery; although the scrap has little inherent value, the Corporatti wishes to reward you for your efforts."

Skeen spoke up. "Although unnecessary, we appreciate that. Transmitting our bank account deposit access info now."

"Funds will be transferred. We are now dispatching drones to take possession of the scrap. Captain Manert, the Admiral passes on her well-wishes and hopes that after the transfer, you and your partner might honor her with attending brunch aboard the *Mutual Wife*."

"Tell the Admiral we'd be more than pleased," Manert said. The communications holo vanished. "Skeen, want to keep an eye on those drones while they grab the sphere? Make sure they don't damage the tether."

"Sure," Skeen said, gesturing for the snack tray to float over to her.

Manert detached himself from the ceiling and settled into his work-a-day body. He started for the door to the bridge. "Come on, Chuck."

Aoki followed, not sure if he was in trouble for speaking out like he had, interrupting the conversation with the enthak. He wasn't generally permitted to speak on the bridge, and certainly not to interfere with things so blatantly.

"Good work back there, Chuck," Manert said, rolling down the hall.

"Thanks," Aoki replied, relieved.

"Saved our lives. Worth a reward. Anything in mind?"

Aoki didn't have to think long. He knew the offer didn't extend to anything so magnificent as his freedom or even a profit-sharing plan. "I'd love some more helmet time. Maybe an hour a day set aside exclusive to it."

"Fifteen minutes, every other day."

"Every day."

"Deal." Manert hung a left. He was heading for the gymnasium.

"No chance of starting now, is there, sir?" Aoki asked.

"Later. I feel like a workout before dinner with the Admiral." Manert slowed, spun his sensor pack around to look at Aoki. "I think today we'll go for four-gees. I'm in a good mood."

"Glad one of us is."

Ten

SALONA REX

BORED OF DEATH AFTER only three hundred short years, Salona resurrected herself as a four-armed, neon-skinned, seventy-foot tall Shiva and set off on a rampage of destruction across the devastated surface of Earth.

The tired old planet having been pounded down to a near uniform desert by time and weather, centuries of concerted nanchine strip-mining to feed her campaigns, and finally countless enemy orbital bombardments, there wasn't much left for Salona to destroy. The ruins of her capital city–walled off behind a pulsing energy dome as a memorial to the trillions that had died by her will–was all they'd left her. All that remained of an empire that once embraced the galaxy, and was, briefly, embraced back.

Her massive palm slapped hard against the shimmering purple of the dome. A flow of microscopic semi-sentient nanchines rushed out from her, through her hand, spreading over the dome. Out to the mile high pylons supporting it.

Infected and quickly overcome by nanchines, the pylons discharged lightning into the starless, eternally night sky. The shifting purple dome winked out, plunged the world into total darkness.

She nodded and stepped into her city. Her third eye snapped awake, flooded the ruins with a divine light.

Her beloved city hadn't changed at all since they'd dragged her from it, forced her voluntary unslumber. Twisted, torn, once glorious, the city had been reduced to indistinct mounds of porous slag by a forty-year long siege capped by a war-ending artificial singularity fired cowardly from an intervening hyper dimension.

Salona bent, thrusting her four hands into the closest mound. Slender fingertips glowed–nanchine skin agitated and restless–slipping easily into the mottled glass and metal slag. She scooped up massive handfuls of what used to be her Ministry of Culture. That, or maybe it was the Ministry of Peace, a tower she wouldn't have recognized intact. It didn't matter now. She raised the handfuls to her face and blew, a great breath, sending a cloud of Ministry out over the city.

Billowing streams of nanchines detached from her fingertips, followed the cloud. Some congealed around the cloud, began their work on the chunks of Ministry as they tumbled back to the ground. Other nanchines fanned out to the rest of the city. The city would be converted within hours, broken down into constituent molecules, prepared for rearrangement.

She felt the enemy's first acknowledgement of her rebirth as little more than a transient, fiery stab between her left shoulder blades. She arched her back, waited for the rest of the volley she'd sensed coming on the horizon even before she'd broken the dome.

They hit her with a hundred micromissles, strafing across her back. Exploding on impact, releasing drillbores intended to puncture her skin and disrupt the electrostatic bonds keeping her nanchines coalesced in Shiva form. The assault should have split her body in two.

But she'd reinforced, shifted extra nanchines around to thicken her skin. Before that first one hit.

She spun just as the second assault was screaming at her through the dispersing smoke of the first.

No micromissiles this time. These were serious weapons, now. Pinwheel nuketips on cluster bomblets, spiraling down at her. Dropped in a flyby of semi-dimensional fighter craft piloted by the nano-animated corpses of her former personnel guard, turned against her. Not willingly turned. They were dead because they'd refused to give her up.

Distressed at the treacherous reward their loyalty to her had bought them, she reflexively swatted her hand through the twirling bomblets, swatting annoying insects. Her hand was torn off in the resulting explosions, nanchines unable to retain cohesion in the firestorm. A stupid mistake, letting her emotions get the better of her, but it played into her plan, and her hand was already reforming. She watched it grow, nanchines welling up into the pulsing stump.

The third assault came as she feigned entrancement in her re-growing hand, as if she'd never seen such a thing before. More bomblets. They shouldn't have knocked her off her feet. But they did. She let them.

She fell forward, collapsed to the earth, four arms spread wide, making no attempt to cushion her crash. The thunderous noise of her fall was drowned out in the nuclear cacophony.

The little ships with their dead pilots wheeled around, descended on her, a swarm of robotic bees with laser stingers out, buzzing viciously. They sunk electrostatic rods deep into her nanchine flesh to paralyze her. Proceeded to cut her apart, rend her.

Her nanchines, those that could, slunk away, scurrying for the protection of the barren earth and dark shadows of the city. It's what she wanted them to do.

She could have fought. Could have resisted. And won.

But winning this fight was not the plan. She had a war to win. And her enemies were going to help her do it.

———————————————

Her core cut free, dumb and blind and smiling patiently in the void, she had been carried upward under a dead man's ship to meet her guards in a complex of machines in the prison shell around the world.

She had half expected instant obliteration. But then her captors were weak, self-important. Of course they would want to talk. If only to try and reform her. Or, more honestly, demonstrate superiority through their supposed mercy.

"Your behavior does not strike us as appreciative."

The warden's voice intruded into the void they'd placed her within. Subdued, harmonious. It disgusted her. "I'm supposed to thank you?"

They'd opened the infospace just enough to converse with her. A sliver, no room for any treachery, no possibility of her taking advantage. Or so they must have thought. She'd figured out how to do many things in those long, dead years.

"We let you live, tyrant."

One of her new tricks, she sent a slice of herself out the way carelessly left open to her, to the shell's local infospace. The enemy wouldn't notice. Their arrogance would not allow them to see her as a threat.

"Live?" She disguised her reach outside herself with a ghostly, sardonic laugh.

"Continue to exist as an entity, then. But you didn't keep your word, did you? You promised to remain dormant."

"Duress." A quiet surge past a sleepy firewall, a writhing twitch of consciousness as key, and the shell's infospace was opened to her. It had been easier than she had dared hoped.

"It was the price to be paid for us allowing you to continue at all."

"Not a fair bargain, I've found." She probed around the shell. Felt the false strength of it, the deceptive complexity of its systems. "I exist, but must remain inactive, dead. Punishment beyond the worst I ever inflicted."

"Disputable. But irrelevant. You will go back to your dormancy willingly? Or must we force you?"

"The bargain still exists?" A few twitches of her mind, and every system on the shell was irreversibly at her command. "I would have thought they'd have become annoyed enough with me by now and simply ended it. Use this as an opportunity to erase me."

"They are concerned, but they are merciful."

And stupid. They actually believed they could contain her, control her. But it was she who was now in control. Of the shell, at least, and soon, if their arrogance held out, much, much more. "They should be concerned."

"Are we to take that as a declaration of intent?"

The sliver of herself probing for the way out found the doorway, almost in the open, barely hidden behind a translation matrix. After finding it, it was a simple matter to break through to the greater infospace, the one of a million worlds, a trillion streams. She simply rode the signal they were using to talk to her. They hadn't even guarded it.

They'd regret that.

Her consciousness touched the galaxy then, and she reeled with pleasure.

The rush of the streams, the contact with so many voices, so much information, after so many years with only her own thoughts as company, it almost overwhelmed her. And what those voices told her reinforced her belief the galaxy still needed her.

"Is silence your answer, tyrant?"

Entropy. She could read it in every stream of the infospace, screaming at her. Unfolding, creeping entropy, soon all-consuming. It would be unnoticed by lesser beings, those without her vision, her vastness. Only she was capable of hearing the sound, recognizing the threat. And only she was capable of doing something about it.

They'd done this. Her warden. Her captors. Her enemy. When she had emerged from death, boredom had motivated her. Now, a new anger drove her.

The time for feigning was over.

Her consciousness struck out. A thousand strands, branching into a million streams. Seized them. She met no resistance at all. "I'm expected then to go back down to the depths? To let you do what you're doing to my galaxy? To ignore my responsibilities?"

"You have no responsibilities. You gave them up."

"They were taken from me."

One strand sunk down. Down to old Earth. Down to her waiting children. She woke them, called them to her.

"Then you agree--"

"I agree only to take them back."

The infospace laid bare to her, she was distressed.

What had they done to her galaxy?

She'd civilized the galaxy. Forged it with a fire of exquisite dominance into a single community. Her vision, her will alone had done this, and she had gone down willingly to defeat knowing the galaxy itself was to be her monument. But the enemy, they had squandered the legacy.

They destroyed her, fought such a hard-bought victory, and for what? Judging by what the galaxy had become since, only to punish her. Not to replace her rule with something better.

Technology had not progressed in her absence. Nothing had. Stagnation. Regression. The infospace laid this bare to her. And the people—the ungrateful, forgetful cattle—they had tranquilly accepted the fate their new rulers had bestowed on them. Trading evolution for peace. They had gone to root. Embraced the rot.

Content in their stagnation.

Unprepared. Unprotected. They needed her again. Needed the fire she had brought to the galaxy. Would bring again.

Swarms of nanchines reaching up from the ruined Earth in shifting tendrils converted the prison shell into a suitable flagship, needle-like and undetectable despite its sheer size. Salona set out for the heart of the enemy. A quick strike was called for, hit and run, to shake them up, to get this started correctly. To declare her return in no uncertain terms and to get them hating her. Hate would drive them.

Emerging from a wormhole opening over the seat of the enemy's governance, her needle ship—fully an extension of her consciousness—dove down into the cluster of connected worldlets with their sprawling, interconnected complexes. Split through them, the skin of the ship flexing out and rending all within its reach. Left a dead hole at the center of realspace, and the infospace. A billion lives scarified to evolution and revenge in an instant, billions of infosystems wiped out and forever lost.

It was glorious. Memorable.

She slipped out another wormhole before the enemy had time to respond. Struck out for the edges of the Way. She attacked randomly, skipping system to system, sparing some, totally annihilating others. Flung moons into worlds, worlds into suns. Her power had never been more refined, absolute. Enjoyable.

She felt the galaxy's collective panic and fear through the infospace. A spreading cacophony. Citizens calling on their beloved leaders to do something, anything. Protect them. What had happened to their peace?

The enemy had no choice but to respond.

Engines of industry and science were unleashed. Restrictions on research lifted. Progress accelerated. She hadn't seen anything like it since the first time.

Yes, they needed her still.

At Jiove they were waiting for her.

———

They'd bathed the system in a newly-developed net which prevented wormholes from opening. But not until she'd wormholed in, trapping her.

Arrayed before her, the massed military might of a roused giant. Countless ships, from microscopic scouts to gas-giant sized sun-destroyers. Crewed by the best humans, post-humans, sentient machines. The system thick with them, all intent on a single mission.

To capture her. And they'd do it, too. They finally had the taste for blood back. It's all she ever wanted for her galaxy. Her gift. Passionate hate. A dagger in the heart of entropy.

She prepared for the fight she'd wanted all along, knowing she'd lose, welcoming it as a mother bird welcomes her children take wing.

But she wouldn't let her children fly by themselves without cost. Entropy was too near, too easy to fall back into. She had to give them a fight. Make them earn their salvation.

She sent configuration commands through the needle ship—grown in size and capability as her campaign rolled on, taking in materials, the spoils of war. One ship became millions, a deadly swarm orbiting her central core.

They came at her, wave after wave, her swarm pulsing to meet them. Firestorms, electromagnetic blasts, the chaos of battle. Ebb and flow. Noble rushes, bold feints.

She destroyed two-thirds of the enemy fleet before it overwhelmed her. A single ship broke through the swarm to pierce her central core.

She flung two singularities kept hidden in a neighboring dimension together, then.

Obliteration, a final blow to the enemy, a final gift to her children. The space-time disruption took the Jiove system, and dozens of surrounding ones, with it. Trillions dead.

She should have gone down into timeless nothingness with them. But that single ship, it had found its mark. Found her. And kept her safe.

"It's over, tyrant."

She knew that voice. The despised voice. Her warden. The enemy. The voice of an old friend.

"Come, now."

She found she could not refuse.

They'd already rebuilt the prison shell when they returned her to her ruined Earth. More defenses this time, more controls, better protection from external or internal intrusion. She had to assume all this. They'd shut her out completely this time, learned their lesson. No sliver to the infospace open to or offered her. They talked–more talk!–to her the old fashioned way.

They manifested her into a biological form, locked her into unconnected flesh. Gave her a face. Ears to listen. Eyes to watch as they bound her to a chair and splayed holograms of her crimes out before her.

Her living monuments, mobilizing, rebuilding their lives. Their peace. But with fresh memories of the threats they must always remain prepared to fight. They'd not slip into stagnation so quickly, this time.

She smiled back at the images with unfamiliar lips.

"You're proud of what you've done, aren't you?"

The warden spoke from somewhere, voice filling the room. The coward, refusing to share the same physical space as her. A smart entity, after all.

"It needed doing." A noise above her, a grinding. She tilted her head to the ceiling, flesh moving slow and heavy. Stared up into blackness. "I am the engine that drives their evolution. They'll see that, come to recognize that they need me, every now and then. To spur them forward. To beat back the entropy."

"They already knew that."

A cylinder descended from the darkness over her, it's tip humming.

She sighed, knowing what was coming. "And yet they did nothing."

"You were allowed to wake in the first place, weren't you?"

They didn't give her a chance to respond. Death came down again.

She waited for their boredom to return.

About the Author

A self-deprecatingly egomaniacal author, doodler and disposable fountain pen owner, J I Greco is uncompromisingly corruptible, intermittently dependable, and endearingly awkward in most social situations.

He was first published in the Spring 1998 issue of Absolute Magnitude Magazine with a short story called "The Road to Wealth". His novels include *Take the All-Mart!*, *Rocketship Patrol*, *Yuki: Licensed Space Pirate*, and *I, Nuthrem*.

He lives in southwestern Ohio and at jigreco.com.

Also by J I Greco